One Wicked Weekend

Fantasies, Inc.

Marie Tuhart

Hot Blooded Press

ONE WICKED WEEKEND

QUALITY CONTROL: We strive to produce error-free books, but even with all the eyes that see the story during the production process, slips get by. So please, if you find a typo or any formatting issues, please let us know at marie@marietuhart.com so that we may correct it.

Thank you!

Blurbs

♥

Cassie

Marcus DeLuca is a problem I don't need–powerful, ruthless, and dangerously addictive. He doesn't ask. He takes. And now he wants me, with no rules and no limits, for one weekend.

I should say no. I should run. Instead, I say yes, because there's something about Marcus I can't resist.

I swore I'd never be vulnerable again, that no man would ever have power over me ever again. Except, I'm falling for him, unable to stop the storm he creates in me.

And I'm terrified, because men like Marcus don't do love. And if I let him in, I risk losing myself. And this time, if I shatter, I'm afraid I'll never recover.

Marcus

I don't lose. And I sure as hell don't beg.

Cassie thinks she can keep me at arm's length. She's wrong. Because she's already mine, even if she doesn't realize it yet. Something is holding her back--it's in her eyes, in the way she tries to distance herself. There's a pain there I need to heal, to make whole.

I dare her to give me a weekend—no limits, no rules, no way out. I'll tempt her. Challenge her. Make her crave me.

I have one weekend to break down her defenses, just one chance to claim every part of her, even the scars.

Because I'm not here for a taste. I'm here for her. And I won't leave without what's mine.

Note to Readers

This book was originally published as His for the Week-end. It has been update and has now become the first book in my new series Fantasies Inc. I want to be transparent this book has been published before. The book has been updated and slightly changed.

Contents

Chapter One

❤

Marcus

I sat back in my chair as Cassie Adams marched into my office, her blue eyes flashing with displeasure. I fought to wipe the smug grin off my face. Finally, some emotion out of her. Satisfaction flowed through my body. Cassie was ready to do battle, all buttoned up with her hair pulled back. Earlier in the day, her hair had been down and two buttons undone. I noticed. I notice everything where she's concerned.

Maybe she was shoring up her defenses. It didn't matter to me. She was mine now.

My intimate gift had the desired effect—her in my office. It didn't escape my notice that she waited until everyone left for lunch to confront me. "Good afternoon, Cassie." I kept my tone even.

"Don't 'good afternoon' me, Marcus DeLuca. I've had enough. This has got to stop and stop now." She stood before my desk, vibrating with what I wanted to believe was unfulfilled desire, but I knew better. She was also irritated.

It didn't matter. She was here.

I'd picked my latest gift with care and the knowledge it would probably push her over the edge, right where I wanted her. I leaned farther back in my leather executive chair to ease the pressure in my groin. "What has to stop?"

I held my amusement in when she stomped her foot and a storm kicked up in those baby blues of hers. It took all my control not to jump out of my chair, push her over my desk, and fuck her. She did that to me—made me lose control—and I didn't like it. I prided myself on my iron-tight control.

"Don't play games with me. The flowers, the notes, and the gifts. It stops now."

The time for teasing was over. She'd thrown down the challenge, and I planned to pick it up. "I made my intentions clear two months ago. I told you the gloves were coming off, and I was going to pursue you until you gave in." I'd made a habit of studying her, to see what made her tick so I could make her mine.

She'd never told me no. I'd respect her wishes if she did. But I suspected she didn't want to and had no idea how to deal with me. Sexual chemistry had arced between us from the first day we first met. I wanted her like I'd wanted no other woman, and I was determined to have her.

"Yes, but..." Her gaze dropped to her feet, a delicate flush coloring her cheeks.

A flash of tenderness welled up in me at her indecision—along with the need to pull her into my arms and comfort her. But at the same time, I wanted to kiss her until she couldn't breathe and fuck her until she screamed my name.

"I can't take this anymore." Her voice was whisper soft, but I heard the words as clear as if she'd shouted them.

My cock jumped. I would prove to her that I was more than just a co-worker, and I planned to show her a relationship between us could work. "What are you willing to give me to stop?"

Her head snapped up, and she gnawed on her lower lip. "Twenty-four hours."

"Not enough. A hundred and twenty." I was willing to negotiate with her, but she wasn't going to get everything her way.

Her mouth opened and then closed. Her gaze darted left, then right, before settling back on my face. I could almost see the wheels turning in her head, trying to figure out her next move.

"Too long. Forty-eight."

I stood and crossed to her. I needed to be close to her as we negotiated this agreement. Little did she know it was only temporary. "Still not enough. Ninety-six uninterrupted hours with you."

Her nose scrunched and her lashes swept down, cutting off my view of her very expressive eyes. "Sixty. From six Friday night until six Monday morning."

I noted the stubborn set of her chin. It wasn't an ideal bargain, but I could live with it. I would not fail in winning her over. Leaning close, I whispered, "I'll take it."

Cassie exhaled, lashes rising until our gazes clashed. "What are the ground rules?"

"There are none."

Her eyes widened. I had her now, and I wasn't letting her go. I held her gaze, my tone hard and commanding. "No barriers. No rules."

Her shoulders dipped, then straightened as if she was preparing for battle. "All right, but when the sixty hours are done, we're finished. I mean it. No flowers, no gifts, no mention of the weekend. Ever."

Without another word, she spun on her heels to leave my office. I hurried across the room and captured her by the shoulders before she made it to the door. I leaned over, my lips brushing her ear, and smelled her fresh scent. "Remember what I said at the party."

Her swift intake of breath was my answer. She did remember.

"You belong to me," I whispered.

"I belong to no man."

I slid my hands down her arms past her clenched fists and encircled her waist, pulling her flush against my body. She didn't struggle, but her breathing grew choppy. I pressed my erect dick against her ass. "You will belong to me, I promise."

"For sixty hours only." She wrenched herself from my embrace and turned her head to glare at me. "That's all you'll get, Marcus. That's all it can be."

"I wouldn't bet on it."

"There are sexual harassment laws you have to abide by."

"Only if you file." A smug smile crossed my lips.

"I will if you make one move toward me after the weekend." Pivoting, she marched out of my office, treating me to her luscious ass as she walked away.

I closed my office door and locked it before returning to my chair. I gently released my zipper and pulled my cock out. It was hard and pulsing. Soon, I'd have Cassie beneath me and then she'd learn the type of man I am.

Chapter Two

♥

Cassie

What in God's name had I done? Made a deal with the devil, that's what. I was shaking, and my pussy throbbed; my breasts tingled, and my breath came way too fast. And none of it was from fear. Only Marcus could make me this aroused without even trying.

I'd made the decision to confront him to get him to back off, not to agree to a no-holds-barred weekend. How did I let myself be talked into that? Actually, we'd negotiated the weekend. But damn it, negotiation was my specialty, especially since I ran the customer service department of Fantasies, Inc. Somehow, he'd outwitted me on this one.

His last words sent a chill through me. I would not be his. I was not a submissive woman like my mother. I was my own woman, in control of myself and my body.

A weekend of sex with Marcus would get him out of my system, then I'd be done.

It would put me in a vulnerable position, but I would keep my guard up. I wouldn't leave myself open to him or anyone. I wouldn't accept pain the way my mother had. I wouldn't give up my hard-fought control. Ever.

Marcus had been a thorn in my side from the day we met, but over the last year, the pain from the thorn had turned into unchecked desire and need, damn it. Not only did he keep me on my toes professionally, but mentally as well.

Was it because my last relationship crashed right before I met Marcus? Or was it because I had talked with Josh, head of the operations department, about how to go about scheduling my own fantasy. No, Josh wouldn't talk to anyone about my asking to become a client. Confidentially was critical to the company and its clients.

Damn, why was I spending so much time analyzing the whys? They didn't matter. Not when my emotions were all over the place and I was having trouble regaining my hard-fought control.

I strode into my office without even realizing how I got there, settled back into my chair, and looked down at my desk. There was only one thing I loved and that was my job.

Fantasies, Inc. was a company that specialized in making sexual fantasies come true. By legal means, of course.

People paid handsomely for their indulgences to become reality. Since the Sexual Freedom Act, companies like ours were no longer taboo. We did have rules and regulations to follow, but the powers that be had never found fault with the company.

Fantasies, Inc. paid well to have the best people work for them, and I was happy to head the customer service department. It took patience some days to listen to the complaints, but mainly the company received compliments.

Marcus was the superman of Research and Development, and from his reporting in the departmental meetings, the R&D was better run than it had been in years.

My phone rang, and I jumped, hitting the white gift box sitting on my desk. I glared at it as I picked up the receiver. "Cassie Adams, how may I help you?"

"Now there's a loaded question." Marcus' whisky-smooth voice flashed through my bloodstream.

I fought against the boneless feeling invading my body at the sound of his voice. *Get ahold of yourself. Control, remember?* "What do you want?"

"I wanted to remind you to bring the present with you this weekend."

My gaze went to the white box. Why hadn't I taken it with me when I went to his office and given it back?

"Sure." What else could I say? I was the one who offered the weekend.

"Good. I can't wait to try those nipple rings on you."

Before I could answer, he hung up. No. No. No. I wasn't wearing them. The teddy, fine, but not the rings. No way.

My nipples tightened in anticipation, regardless of what my mind thought. I wasn't adverse to sexual play, but memories flooded in. A time when I was a teenager and exploring my own sexuality and I'd found a set of nipple rings in the bathroom. My parents had been very open about sex... My lashes drifted shut.

Keep breathing. In and out. In and out. Pain swamped me. I hadn't known they would hurt so much when I clipped them on. I fought against the memory and breathed deeply until I regained control.

I would keep my control this weekend, even if it killed me. There could be nothing between Marcus and myself. I wouldn't allow it. I couldn't allow it.

***

Friday morning arrived faster than I wanted. Marcus had been true to his word: No more presents had arrived, at least not yet. Today was the day. I took my normal seat at the back of the small table where we held staff meetings.

Our President, John Boyd, sat at the head of the table. To his right was the head of Technology, Asher, financial head, Lucas, then me, and to his left sat Miles, head of HR. Also Josh and Dean, who ran Operations. Marcus wasn't here yet.

He sauntered in and took the seat next to mine, and I fought against sighing as he pushed his chair closer.

"Let's get started." John glanced around the table. "Cassie, customer service?"

I shifted in my chair to get away from the heat coming from Marcus. The man was like a furnace. "No complaints, mainly compliments."

"Good. Asher?"

"The new software system is on track to be installed in a few months, and I've scheduled an onsite consultant to make the tweaks we're going to need."

I'd forgotten about the new software system. That was not going to be fun. I hated changes like that.

"Great job. Are there any issues you can see at this point in time?" John asked.

"Not yet. Once we start tweaking the program, that's when we'll find the bugs."

John nodded. "Miles?"

"All is well in HR. The coffee shop downstairs is doing well, and everyone likes it. I'll be extending their contract."

My grin was automatic. The coffee shop had been Miles' idea. The woman who ran it was an independent contractor. She paid for the spot and ran the shop, but she and her employees had to be vetted by HR.

"They serve the best pastries," Lucas piped up.

"Let's hear your update, Lucas."

"I've been going over the financials of the company you want to bring into the Fantasies, Inc. fold."

"Problem?" asked John.

"Not sure yet. I'm searching for a forensic accountant to take a look. I can't put my finger on it, but something doesn't seem right."

"Very well. Keep me informed. We have a few months before we have to make a hard decision." John looked at Josh and Dean.

"Operations are going quite well," said Josh.

"I have nothing to add," said Dean.

I glanced at Josh, and he winked at me. Since our conversation, I couldn't help smiling at him. While we were technically in different departments, finding out more about Operations made my job in customer service easier.

A hand landed on my knee, and my gaze swung to a scowling Marcus. I didn't think; I reached over, grabbed his crotch, and squeezed. Hard. His eyes widened, and he removed his hand from my knee.

"Marcus?"

"R&D is working on some new things. I have a few that need to be tested yet, but I should have them ready to demo for everyone in a few months."

"If you need a test subject, let me know," said Dean.

Everyone laughed. But Marcus' husky laugh swept over my skin like a spring breeze.

"All right. Seems like everyone is doing well, and there are no complaints. Everything is on schedule for the company, and I'm happy with the revenue we're producing. I like staff meetings like this. We're done until the next one." John stood and left the room.

I scooted my chair back and stood. Marcus did the same thing. Before I could move, he leaned over and whispered, "Nipple rings."

Heat flared, and my breath stuttered in my chest. Without looking back, I walked out of the conference room. Normally, I'd stay and chat, but not today. I didn't need to be in Marcus' presence any more than necessary. I was going to spend the weekend with him. That was all. My stomach quivered.

***

I stared at the clock. Four. I was barely holding on to my control. The white box I'd shoved into my desk drawer had taunted me all week. I really should be able to ignore it, but today, especially after Marcus' comment, I was constantly opening and closing the drawer.

Damn it. I opened the drawer again, but this time, I pulled the box out. It was late enough in the day I shouldn't be disturbed. I opened the pristine white lid. Pushing the midnight blue teddy aside, I lifted the smaller velvet box and opened it.

I stared at the two gold nipple rings before I pulled them out. I held them in my palm, admiring their smooth metal and their light weight. These looked nothing like the ones I'd found in my childhood bathroom.

Those had been round and made of heavy steel with little spikes on the inside. These were more like actual rings and would easily slip onto my sensitive nipples. My nipples were already erect thinking about using these. Damn. I should have tried them out so I'd know. Too late now.

How would these gold rings feel on my skin?

My pussy tightened as anticipation flowed through my blood. I could picture Marcus standing before me, his fingers playing with my breasts before he slipped the rings over my taut nipples. My breath caught in my throat as my pussy moistened.

Stop this!

I started to put the rings back into their box when a click of the door captured my attention. My head jerked up. Marcus stood with his back against the wooden door to my office, an ultra-satisfied grin on his face.

"How…" I cleared my throat to get the words out. "How long have you been standing there?" I had no idea why I didn't notice him come in.

"Long enough." He pushed away from the door and marched toward me.

I dropped the rings back into their box and shoved it into the bigger box. "Is there something I can help you with?" I cursed silently the second the words left my mouth. Talk about putting your foot into your mouth. Give Marcus an opening and he'd pounce.

His green eyes lit up. The infuriating man had taken my words as an invitation. Damn. How could I stop this?

"There is something you can help me with." He stalked around my desk.

My pulse kicked up a notch. "Marcus." I rose to my feet.

"Put them on." His voice was low and firm and sent shivers up my spine.

"Later." Much later. Maybe never.

His green eyes darkened. "Now." This time there was a command in his voice.

My hand hovered above the box. I shook my head as I realized what I was doing and forced my hand to drop. I was not like my mother; I wasn't going to mindlessly obey a man.

"Our time hasn't begun yet."

Strong masculine hands closed over mine. His skin wasn't soft, but rough enough to send shivers along my nerves and remind me he was all man.

"Put them on." His voice dropped to a husky whisper that stroked my skin like velvet fingers. "You know you want to. Think about how they will feel against your skin. How they will cause your nipples to harden and rub against your bra, making your breasts more sensitive. When I take them in my mouth, you'll cry out with pleasure."

I pried my hands from beneath his to grab the edge of my desk before my knees gave out. The images his words invoked caused my pussy to spasm and my nipples to tighten into hard buds. If he could do that with words, how was I going to survive his touch? Without saying another word, he lifted the lid on the box.

He pulled the smaller box out and cradled it in his large hands. A small earthquake shot through my body. How would those hands feel on my skin? In my hair? Stroking my pussy until I climaxed? My mind went blank.

His long fingers toyed with the top button of my blouse as our gazes locked. I held my breath as he undid the first button and paused. He was waiting for me to say yes, but I wasn't ready to give him that kind of power yet, so I remained silent. Marcus grinned and undid the next button.

So much for permission.

When he undid the third button, I muttered, "I didn't say you could continue."

His gaze met mine. "When you agreed to the weekend, you gave me permission to touch you."

True. I hadn't thought of that when his palms skimmed over my neck. Awareness flowed through my body.

He didn't stop, slipping his hands under the fabric and pushing it down my arms, trapping them against my sides and baring my lace-covered breasts to the cool office air.

My skin tingled at his light touch, and my breathing grew shallow. I should stop him. We were at work. "Marcus—"

"So beautiful," he whispered, his breath brushing my cheek. "I knew they'd be." He shook his head as if trying to clear his mind. "If you're going to object, now is your last chance."

I opened my mouth, but no words came out. The heat in his gaze and the need coursing through my body kept me mute. His palms covered my breasts as lava exploded in my blood, and I fought against letting out a needy moan.

Next thing I knew, he'd maneuvered me so my ass rested against my desk, and his chest brushed my sensitive, lace covered breasts.

I finally found my voice. "This is a bad idea." We were in my office and anyone could walk in. What was I thinking letting this go so far? That's the problem. I wasn't thinking. My brain had short-circuited the second he touched me.

"This is the best idea I've had in a while." With deft fingers, he undid the front clasp of my bra. My breasts spilled out as the lacy cups peeled away.

I tried to lift my hands, but they were trapped by my clothing. Damn it. "Marcus." I called his name again, making my voice as firm as possible, but it came out soft and filled with need.

The rings he'd taken from the box rolled around in his palm with a metal *twang*, echoing through my office. God, I wanted his bare hands on my breasts, caressing them, making me ache for his touch.

"Let me tell you about these little beauties." He leaned forward, his breath caressing my cheek. "I created these to give a woman pleasure. That's why I love R&D; I can create things for pleasure, both giving and receiving."

He spoke of pleasure, not pain. How could that be right? His thumb brushed over my nipple, a tremor sweeping through my body. He did the same to the other nipple, causing the same reaction. My pussy clenched as my skin heated with pleasure.

No. I couldn't do this. Not here. Not yet. I glanced up, and my gaze clashed with his. "Stop. Now."

His gaze hardened, but he removed his hands from my breasts. I took a deep breath. I'd been afraid he wouldn't listen to me, and he'd continue regardless of my wishes. He didn't say a word, but his gaze never left my face as he fastened my bra, slid my blouse back onto my shoulders, and re-buttoned it.

"We'll try these out, later." He replaced the nipple rings in their box. "Actually, I'll take them with me. I'll see you at six." Stepping back, he walked out of my office.

I collapsed into my chair, heart pounding.

Dear God. I raised my trembling hand to my chest. Marcus had listened to me. I'm not sure if that made me happy or sad, but he'd listened.

It was more than him stopping when I asked—it was my reaction to his touch, the excitement of anticipation that swept through me when he touched me.

Fire burned low in my belly, and my pussy throbbed with unfulfilled desire. If I reacted this way, and my reaction wasn't one I was expecting, how would I get through the weekend with him? I couldn't back out of the weekend. I'd given my word, and I didn't renege on my word. Plus once it was done, that would be it. He'd leave me alone; that was the deal.

Why did I have the unsettling feeling my life was spiraling out of control?

Chapter Three

♥

Marcus

It was six-twenty. Cassie wasn't going to show. I shook my head, unable to believe she'd stood me up. I paced around the dark wood-paneled security room, disappointment filling me.

Pausing, I looked at the security monitors for the hundredth time. I'd pushed her earlier, in her office, but only because I was aware that, if I didn't, she'd retreat and hide behind that layer of coolness of hers. I thought I'd have the weekend to convince her we belonged together.

I sat down and continued to stare at the monitor showing my security gate. Did I regret pushing her? Maybe a bit. I'd watched her enough to know that a very sensual woman was alive and kicking inside. From the gentle sway of her hips to the small smile that hovered around her lips to the flirty tone she'd take when talking to other men. But today, I saw something else.

Fear. What happened in her past that made her afraid? Fear that had increased as I touched her. Who hurt her? I'd get answers this weekend.

Damn. Was that why she wasn't coming? No, I didn't believe that. I'd seen her in action, and my Cassie wasn't a coward. She'd taken on other managers in the office who talked down to her or made lewd jokes and never batted an eyelash.

The ringing of a bell startled me. I blinked, not sure I should believe the monitor. A small, gunmetal gray SUV, with a very harassed-looking Cassie behind the wheel, idled at the gate.

My palms were damp with anticipation. Wiping them on my pants, I pressed the button for the security gate. I hit several keys on the keyboard so each camera followed her progress. I zoomed in the focus, giving me a closer view of her face.

She was stressed. I could see it in the tightness of her mouth, the way her brows were scrunched up, and the way her fingers gripped the steering wheel.

Was she nervous? Afraid? Aroused? It could be any of those. I watched as the security gate closed and Cassie pulled up to the front of the house. I left the security room to go greet my guest. We needed to talk, first and foremost. Once I talked with her, I'd know how to proceed tonight. The last thing I wanted was a woman who was scared.

Chapter Four

♥

C assie

I took a deep breath for probably the thousandth time. A last-minute problem had tied me up at the office, and by the time I finished, ran home, and packed my bag—yes, I waited until the last minute—I knew I'd never make it to Marcus' home by six.

While driving, I cursed him for not giving me a phone number. I drove as fast as I dared on unfamiliar roads.

I stopped my hybrid SUV in front of the house in the circular driveway and stared out the windshield. When Marcus called before quitting time to give me his address, he hadn't mentioned how far out of town he lived. Of course the phone call I received after his was the problem.

What am I doing here? The answer hadn't changed since the last time I asked myself the question, a whole five minutes ago. *Doing what I've wanted to do for the past year—have sex with a man who has dominated my dreams and fantasies.*

A sliver of fear held me back. Not fear of Marcus but of myself. I refused to believe I was like my mother, submissive to the point of letting my partner do whatever he wanted, no matter what. But wasn't that what had happened in my office earlier today? Hadn't I been ready to submit?

I shook my head. No, I hadn't submitted. I told him to stop. I was in control. And that was the only way I would get through this weekend. Making sure I did the one thing I was good at—control. If I could control my emotions, everything would work out.

My mother had no place in my head this weekend. Pushing the depressing thoughts away, my gaze settled on Marcus' home.

The front door remained closed. Was he waiting for me to ring the bell?

I can't sit out here all night.

Exiting the vehicle, I snagged my bag from the passenger seat, slammed the door a little harder than I should have, and used the key fob to lock it.

Striding up the walkway, I realized Marcus was very security conscious. I'd seen the cameras at the gate and counted at least two cameras and five sets of flood lights from the gate to the front of his house.

The arched entryway was impressive. It looked as if it was made of marble, and the size… I wondered why Marcus owned such a large house. He'd never struck me as a person into material possessions.

But then, what did I really know about him? The man was straightforward and honest, a hard worker, and sexy as hell. From day one he'd been direct with me, making no bones about wanting me. Even after he left my office today, he'd emailed his latest physical from his doctor, showing he was free from any sexually transmitted diseases.

I'd done the same—not that it mattered to me, since it had been well over a year since I last had sex that wasn't with my vibrator. But Marcus had a right to know.

The heavy wooden door swung open when my feet hit the porch. Out of the corner of my eye, I spotted yet another camera perched in the alcove.

Marcus stood there, and my heart contracted. His dark hair was a mess, and his arms were crossed over his chest. While his stance screamed anger, I could've sworn there was a glimmer of relief in his green eyes. But I dismissed it.

"Sorry, I'm late." As the words rushed out of my mouth I wondered why I was apologizing. *No more being sorry.*

Unlike my mother, I wasn't going to apologize for everything.

"I figured you stood me up."

"I gave my word, and I would never go back on that. But
if you'd like, I can leave." I took a step back.

"No." He grasped my forearm, his hold gentle, and took
my bag with his free hand. "Welcome to my home." He
guided me inside and then kicked the door shut. The lock
engaged automatically.

Calm down. He's locked the door; that's all.

My heart jumped. "You live pretty far out."

"I value my privacy." His hands curved around my
shoulders as he spoke, and his green gaze captured mine.
"Plus, it's better not to have neighbors close. No one will
call the police when they hear you scream."

I swayed on my feet as my senses went on full alert. The
fear I'd been pushing aside sprang back full force. Had I
made a terrible mistake? Was Marcus like my father?

My bag hit the floor. Warm palms cupped my cheeks as
Marcus' thumbs swept over my parted lips.

"I can see you misunderstood me. You'll scream in pleasure. I'm not into pain, giving or receiving. Pleasure is all I
want to give you."

My breath rushed out. "You had me worried." My heart
rate was slowing down and my muscles relaxing.

"I saw it in your eyes." An unusual light flickered in his, but it was gone before I could figure out what it meant. "Let's get you settled, then we'll have dinner."

"Dinner?" Confusion ran riot through my mind. Only a few hours ago, he couldn't wait to get his hands on me. Now he wanted to feed me first?

"We need to eat." He released me, picked up my bag, and curved his free arm around my waist to guide me up the winding staircase. "I suspect you missed lunch."

Heat swept into my cheeks. Of course I had. I'd been in his office shortly before lunch today, then Josh had wanted to talk to me about a client request. Lunch was a luxury my workday didn't often afford.

My feet glided over the highly polished hardwood stairs. At the top, Marcus guided me to an open door on the right.

I jolted to a halt. He squeezed my waist before continuing into the room with my bag. A bedroom? Of course, and it was probably his. I wasn't sure I would call this a simple bedroom, though.

I crossed the threshold. The room seemed larger than my apartment. The bed took up almost one entire wall, the cherry frame gleaming in the evening spring light from the huge picture window across the room.

What a view of the mountains you would have from that bed, every day and night. With a quick glance, I noticed the small sitting area with a love seat, but the walls were bare of pictures. The room was immaculate—either Marcus was very neat or he had a housekeeper.

"I've made room in the dresser for you, also in the closet if you want to hang anything up." He gestured to a door I assumed was the closet.

We were going to share a room? Of course we were. I mentally smacked myself. Sex. That's what this weekend was about, nothing more and nothing less. No emotions. Control.

He sat my bag on the bed, and our gazes met. "Unpack and freshen up if you want. I'll be downstairs finishing up dinner. You have ten minutes until it's ready." His long strides had him standing in front of me before I realized he'd moved. "The dining room is on the left from the bottom of the stairs. Please don't be late." His index finger brushed over my lips before he strode out of the room.

Confusion ran through my mind. Why wasn't he taking me to bed right away? I'd fully expected him to jump my bones the second I entered his home. He hadn't. Why not? Nothing was making sense right now. Earlier today, he couldn't keep his hands off me, but now he was playing it calm and cool. I rubbed my temple.

I couldn't figure out Marcus' thoughts. I was usually pretty good at reading body language. When I arrived, he'd seemed angry, but his actions since were gentle and kind. He confused me, and I didn't like it one bit.

I blew out a breath. Okay, all I needed to do was keep a lid on my emotions and get through the weekend. Having a controlling, dominant man like Marcus in my life wasn't a possibility. I picked up my bag and went to the bathroom door. Whoops, that was the walk-in closet. I moved to the other door. Maybe splashing some cold water on my face would help me pull myself back together. I needed to keep my wits about me so I could deal with the everchanging Marcus.

Chapter Five

♥

Marcus

I walked into the kitchen, fighting the need to hightail it back upstairs, throw Cassie onto my bed, and sink into her wet pussy. I wanted her, have for such a long time, but I had to hold back. This weekend was too important not to.

When I opened the front door and saw the fear in her eyes and how tense she was, I changed my plan of action. My anger at her lateness dissipated the second I saw her fear. What in her past was making her so wary?

I put a pot of water on the stove before I walked into the dining room and checked the table settings I'd set up earlier for dinner. Everything was good, but it helped me to do something as I thought about Cassie.

There was something about her that called to me on an emotional level. A connection I'd never felt with another woman. Yes, I wanted her; that was a given. And from her reaction earlier today, she wanted me, too, but something held her back.

Was she afraid of sex?

I shook my head. No, I didn't think it was that, considering she worked for a sex fantasy company.

Was she afraid of me?

My gut clenched. I had never given her a reason to be afraid of me, not that I was aware of.

Had some man hurt her in the past? I'd checked before asking her out. Her last relationship went south a little over a year ago. If he'd hurt her—

My fingers curled into fists. If some man had hurt her, I'd hunt him down and teach him a few things. No one hurt my Cassie. I was already thinking of her as mine. I'd thought of her as mine since I met her over a year ago.

I slowly released the tension in my hands, letting go of anger at something I had no control over. Cassie had to know that I would never hurt her.

Or did she?

I pondered the question. I'd shown my anger earlier, and she'd reacted in fear.

I checked the wine glasses, plates, and candles. Everything was in its place—except my dick. It had hardened the second I opened the door. It was out of control, but then again, I never had much control over my cock around Cassie. I'd wanted her for over a year now, and I wasn't used to denying myself.

Striding over to the digital player, I pushed several buttons, and soft jazz filled the air. Jazz always helped me relax. Tonight I needed it. I would show Cassie she had nothing to fear, because I wanted to give her pleasure. Pleasure I was sure she hadn't known before.

Soft footsteps on the hardwood floor got my attention. Cassie stood in the doorway of the dining room, her rosy lips parted and what looked like amazement on her face. Was her wonderment over my home or the way I set the table? I was happy to see that she'd taken her hair down and let it float around her shoulders. She'd changed out of her business suit and into a soft-looking, lounging-type outfit that complemented her eyes. I was happy, and I wanted her to feel at home and comfortable.

"Come, sit down." I walked across the room and pulled out one of the cherry chairs for her. "Dinner is almost ready."

She glided over and sat. When I leaned over to help push her chair in, I caught a whiff of honey and cream. I inhaled. My cock leapt behind the zipper of my jeans. Later, I promised. Later, I'd bury my dick in her until her scent covered me completely.

With iron will, I backed away and picked up the bottle of white wine. She nodded when I held it up, so I poured her a glass. "I believe you prefer white over red? If this isn't to your liking, let me know. I have other wines."

She nodded, but otherwise sat still as a statue, looking more uncomfortable by the second. I was determined to help her relax.

"I'll be right back with dinner." I didn't wait for her answer and bolted to the kitchen like a nerdy boy with a crush on the head cheerleader. What the hell was wrong with me? Control. I needed control. Willing my cock to calm down, I plated the meal and looked things over once more to ensure it was all perfect. Fruti de mare over pasta e olio, asparagus and pine nut salad, and a loaf of perfect Italian bread. Chardonnay was already on the table.

The chocolate soufflé was in the oven on low heat and would be ready by the time we finished dinner. Perfect seduction by food. A smile curved my lips as I picked up the tray and carried it into the dining room.

Cassie leaned back in her chair, looking more relaxed than before. She sipped her wine and lightly swayed to the music. This was a much better start to the weekend.

"Dinner is served, my lady." I set the tray down and took my seat to her right.

She set her wine glass down, and her mouth opened into an "O" as I set the salad bowl in front of her. "You cooked?"

"Yes." I fought against laughing. "What did you expect?"

"I figured you had someone who cooked and cleaned for you."

"Clean, yes. Cook, no. I enjoy cooking. Eat up." I picked up my fork and watched her do the same.

She speared a small piece of asparagus and other vegetables and lifted it to her lips. Her eyes closed as she chewed. A light moan left her lips. My cock shifted, and I willed it to calm down. It pleased me that she enjoyed the food.

"This is delicious, and I usually don't like cold veggies. What did you do to it?"

I smiled. Outside of my R&D work, cooking was a passion of mine. "Sautéed the asparagus with pine nuts and olive oil." My tense muscles began to relax. I'd wanted to make a good impression with the food, and I had. Happiness filled my soul. "You have to let it cool completely, then add spinach and toss with more olive oil and a hint of white wine vinegar. Then into the fridge to chill."

"Delicious." She took another bite, and my dick throbbed, wanting those lips closing around it and not some hunk of spinach.

"Where did you learn to cook?" she asked.

"College." I picked up my wine glass and leaned back. "I was tired of eating out or getting pizza, so I took one of the university's cooking classes."

"If this is any indication, you excel at it."

She flashed me a grin, and my cock hardened farther. Down, boy.

"Naturally." I fought against my reaction. I wanted her calm and relaxed, to show her I wasn't a threat, because I wasn't. I was just a man who wanted to make all her fantasies come true. Every single one of them, over and over again.

Chapter Six

♥

Cassie

I sipped the white wine, savoring the light, sweet flavors sliding down my throat. It helped keep my confusion under wraps. Marcus had cooked for me. This didn't fit the picture I had of him as the wild bachelor who took a different woman to bed every night, and this wasn't the way I thought the weekend would start out.

I glanced at the covered plates on the tray and wondered what other surprises he had for me. I wasn't picky but I did have some dislikes. The heavenly scent wafting from the plates made my mouth water.

I dabbed my lips with the napkin. "You're not eating."

"I find I'm not hungry for food."

I held my breath when he leaned forward, but all he did was remove my empty salad bowl and replace it with the covered plate. With a flourish, he lifted the lid.

Pasta with shrimp. My stomach grumbled as the delicious scent filled the air. How did he know I loved shrimp? Without hesitation, I picked up my fork and dug in. Marcus stared at me, but I ignored him. Besides, I was hungry. The pasta melted on my tongue. I wasn't a bad cook, but my pasta never tasted like this.

"You like?" There was a hint of amusement in his voice.

"Love it. You're a great cook. My pasta always sticks together or is tough."

"Add a little olive oil to the water when it boils—it helps stop the sticking. As for the toughness..." He leaned forward as I set my fork down. "You're not cooking it long enough. Everything is better when it simmers for a while."

By the heat in his gaze, he wasn't just talking about cooking. Was that why he wasn't rushing me into bed, because he wanted our need for each other to simmer for a while? I picked up my wine glass and sipped before sitting back in my chair. What would he do if I suggested we head to the bedroom? "What was your major in college?"

Chicken, a small voice inside me whispered. I wasn't chicken, but self-preservation was still an option.

A grin played around his lips, as if he knew what I was thinking. "Engineering."

"No wonder you like R&D so much."

His laughter caressed my every nerve, the rich husky sound warming my skin.

"The R&D job at Fantasies, Inc. was made for me." He refilled our wine glasses before lounging back in his seat again. "Tell me how you came to work there."

"I was bored in my last job and saw the online ad for a customer service manager. I applied and got the job."

"And what did you do before that?"

I exhaled. I didn't want to get into this, but I was the one who opened the door, so now I needed to shut it. I waved my hand in the air. "Too many jobs to go into. What about you?"

A smile crossed his lips, but it wasn't one of those nice smiles. It was his wolfish *I'll get you, my pretty* grin, as if he knew exactly what I was doing.

I forced myself to breathe normally, hoping he wouldn't hear my racing heart. *Stay calm. Stay in control.*

His forefinger traced the rim of his wine glass. "I worked with several engineering firms after I graduated college. When Fantasies, Inc. started up, I saw the potential and came aboard right away."

"So you've been with the company since the beginning?" The company was only five years old.

"Yes. John and I are old friends from our college days."

What? I blinked. He was friends with the President/CEO of the company? If this weekend went sideways, he could get me fired without cause. My hand twitched, causing the wine to slosh near the rim.

Warm fingers closed over mine. "Easy. I don't abuse the friendship. You have nothing to fear."

"How..." A ping sounded, and I jumped. I needed to calm down.

"You have a very expressive face. Time for dessert." Releasing my hand, he stood, picked up the plates, and strode into the kitchen.

Get a hold of yourself. I had no idea my face was expressive. I would need to be careful to school my features around him or he'd find out all my secrets.

When he returned, the scent of rich chocolate assaulted me. *Damn, I'm in trouble now.* He set the confection in front of me, and my stomach somersaulted. A chocolate soufflé. Perfectly cooked. A scoop of vanilla ice cream melted on top, and sliced strawberries decorated the edge.

"Are you trying to seduce me with food?" I glanced up at Marcus. His twinkling green eyes met my gaze.

"And if I am?"

"I'd say it's working." Now why did I blurt that out?

"Eat up before your ice cream completely melts."

I picked up my spoon and dug in. My eyes closed in ecstasy on the first bite. Not just vanilla ice cream. French vanilla, along with chocolate heaven. I couldn't suppress the moan that escaped my lips on the second bite.

"Where did you grow up?"

The rich dessert caught in my throat, and I started coughing. Marcus started to rise, but I waved him back into this seat. I picked up my water glass and took a deep drink. How the hell should I answer that question?

Chapter Seven

♥

Marcus

I kept my gaze on Cassie. What was going on in that brain of hers? I asked her a simple question. She did give a lot away in her body language and facial expressions, but there were still missing pieces to the puzzle. I waited until she recovered her breath. "Are you okay?"

"Yes."

Her voice was a little raspy.

"Do I need to repeat the question?"

"No." She pushed back from the table but didn't rise. She rubbed her arms as if she was cold. "Why did you ask where I grew up?"

Interesting that Cassie answered my question with one of her own. Why didn't she want to answer? "I'm interested in all things Cassie." Curiosity filled me. Why was she hiding her past from me?

"I thought this was about sex."

I threw my head back and laughed—I couldn't help it. This woman was precious. She thought that's all this weekend was about? Cassie had a lot to learn about me, and I was looking forward to all of it.

"It's not funny." She rose.

"Cassie." The hurt in her eyes cut my laughter short. Before she could take a step, I rose, moved in front of her, and placed my hands on her shoulders. I fought against the need to drag her into my embrace and hold her.

"This isn't going to work." Her voice was soft. "I never should have made this bargain."

I tightened my hold on her when she tried to move away from me.

"I can't do this." Her voice was barely above a whisper.

"You can." I gave in to the need coursing through my body. I slid my hands down her arms until I found her waist, holding her loosely. Cassie tilted her head, and our gazes met. Her eyes were clouded and confused.

For the first time since I made this bargain, I wasn't sure how to put Cassie at ease with me. A sense of failure started to creep up my spine. No. I wouldn't fail. I would never fail again—once was enough.

"Marcus, I..."

"*Shh.*" I brushed my lips over hers, tracing the seam of her mouth with my tongue before I pulled back. "This weekend is about so much more than sex."

Unable to help myself, I closed my lips over hers again. This time, her lips parted, and I dove in. The taste of warm chocolate teased my taste buds. Her hands moved to my shoulders and then tangled in my hair, pulling me closer. I wanted nothing more than to strip those clothes off her and find her wet core.

Patience. Her tongued dueled with mine, but I softened the kiss. I would make her comfortable. I pulled back from her luscious lips to gaze at her face. Her eyes were still closed, her breathing rapid, and her fingers still buried in my hair.

I forced my own need aside. I wanted to keep things light until Cassie was ready, but it wouldn't be easy. She was so damn sensual. Nothing with her was easy. Cassie was a complicated woman, a woman who hid herself from others. I refused to let her hide from me any longer.

"If it's not about sex, then what is it about?" Her breath brushed against my sensitive skin.

"It's about two consenting adults learning more about each other, exploring each other, and enjoying each other."

"Then by all means, let's enjoy ourselves." She pressed against me, and my cock grew harder.

"Soon." She wasn't going to make this easy on me.

"Don't you want me?" Her voice held a sultry tone. She wiggled, and my cock jerked, seeking her warmth. I bit back a groan. How had she turned the tables on me? When had I lost control of this situation?

"I want you." I kissed her hard and fast before I pried her arms from around my neck and took a step back. Control. I was in control.

I held her hands loosely until her eyes grew wide, and the sensual haze in them lifted. "Oh, God." Her cheeks turned a lovely shade of red as she stepped back. "I never...I mean... Oh, hell. I don't mean to tease you."

I bit back a chuckle. She was about to panic, and I didn't want that. "Why don't you go upstairs and relax while I clean up from dinner."

"Umm. Sure." She spun and all but ran out of the room.

Oh, yes, this was going to be fun.

Chapter Eight

♥

C assie

Stupid. Crazy. Slut.

My father's voice echoed in my head as I sank down on the bed in Marcus' bedroom. He'd said those words to me and my mother daily. Maybe he was right. What the hell had happened to me a few minutes ago?

You're just like your mother. There was my father's menacing voice again. No! I forced the voice away. I was not like my mother. I would never be like her. But the fear remained inside me, eating slowly at my confidence.

Taking a deep breath, I closed my eyes and let my mind wander back to what had happened downstairs. What kind of game was Marcus playing? Or was he? Consenting adults learning about each other, exploring each other, enjoying themselves—that's what he'd said.

I didn't want him to learn about my past. I could handle the exploring and enjoyment, and that was it. Sex, pure and simple, was the best way to silence the voices in my head. My heart fluttered.

Marcus wanted to know what made me tick. I wouldn't allow that to happen. This weekend was simply to get Marcus out of my system so I could move on. That's what we agreed to, and I was going to hold him to that agreement.

Surging to my feet, I crossed the room. A shower would make me feel better, so I stepped into the bathroom and undressed. I turned, slid the shower door open, and stopped. This wasn't a shower; it was a lavish paradise.

He had not one, but three different shower heads. Two hand-held and one rain water type. I flipped the handle, and water came out of the big hand-held. I pinned my hair up and checked the water temperature before stepping inside.

The warmth surrounded me, and my shoulders relaxed. I needed this. I was so keyed up. Was this weekend with Marcus really going to be that bad? I grabbed the bottle of shower gel and squirted some in my hand.

No, I would make the best of this weekend—as much as I could. It was a few days and then Marcus and I would be over. I slid my soapy hands over my body. My nipples perked up. What would his touch be like?

Soft or firm? I pinched my nipple, sending a zing of arousal to my clit. Yeah, that was it. He'd be both soft and firm. I moved my hands down over my belly, to the top of my mound.

I shifted my feet as I dipped a finger between my labia. I gently caressed my clit before slipping a finger in my pussy. I closed my eyes as I stroked myself. How long had it been since I pleasured myself? A while.

Maybe that's why I was primed and ready. I slipped a second finger inside myself, stroking slowly. Would Marcus go slow or fast? My eyes opened. Enough.

This wasn't the time to fantasize. Later, once this weekend ended. Right now, I needed to be ready for Marcus. To shore up my shields, so to speak. The man wouldn't know what hit him. Because I was going to be in control.

Shutting the shower off, I stepped out and wrapped my body in a soft white towel. I wouldn't be caught in a towel. Nope. My defenses were coming back online. I'd show him who he was dealing with.

Chapter Nine

♥

Cassie

My heart pounded at the sound of Marcus' solid footfalls against the wooden floors. The shower had been refreshing, but now my nerves were getting the best of me. I'd had lovers before, but I'd never played the seductress.

Hell, I hadn't even brought the right clothes. I couldn't find the teddy he'd sent me. I remembered having it in bedroom when I packed. I was sure I packed it. Then I remembered the white box was sitting on my dresser. The oversized T-shirt wasn't exactly seducing material, but I couldn't greet him naked. Nope, that wasn't me, and he'd see right through my ploy in a half-second if I did that. Instead, here I was in his bed with the covers pulled up.

Maybe the covers were not a good idea. I needed to show some skin, but before I could lower the material, he entered the room. His gaze settled on me, and a smile played around his lips. Heat filled my veins, and my nipples tightened.

"I like the sight of you in my bed."

"That's good, since we're going to be spending a lot of time here."

"We might." He rubbed his chin while he stared at me. "I'm going to take a shower. The TV remote is on the nightstand."

I stared at his back as he made his way into the bathroom. What the hell was wrong with him? I was sitting here, with only a T-shirt and panties on, waiting in his bed, and...

I blew out a breath. There was nothing wrong with what he was doing; he probably wanted to be fresh and clean. But still he acted like it's nothing unusual to have me in his bed.

Maybe for him it wasn't, but for me... My fist hit the mattress. *Damn the man.* He was destroying my control, and he did it easily. I wanted him in this bed, taking me the way I chose. Fast and hard. Then we could get on with the weekend without this first time hanging over my head.

Reaching out, I snagged the remote and hit the power button. A large flat-screen TV lowered from the ceiling. Men and their toys. The screen flickered to life as Marcus strode into the room wearing a pair of black boxers. Damn, that was a quick shower. I hadn't even heard the water come on.

I stared at him. His black hair was slicked back. My mouth watered at the sight of his muscular chest, trim waist, long strong legs, and damned if I couldn't see his cock bounce with each step he took. I licked my lips.

"Anything in particular you want to watch?" He settled next to me on the bed and took the remote from my now lifeless fingers.

"No. Whatever you want." *Breathe. Don't drool.* Oh, but there was so much to drool over. Marcus was one fine male specimen. Six-pack abs, a chest to die for, shoulders I ached to touch, and...

His cock pressing hard against the fabric of his boxers?

My pussy throbbed with need. This was not good. Not at all. I closed my eyes, trying to find my control. It wasn't working. I wanted to jump his bones.

His arm brushed mine. His heat called to me. I threw back the covers and jumped out of bed.

"Are you okay?" He glanced at the empty spot next to him.

"No." I marched across the room and stood by the window. Frustration filled my veins. Why wasn't this going like I wanted?

"Nervous?"

I shook my head. It wasn't nervousness causing my upset. I was out of sorts. Off-balance. I'd had lovers before, but those times had been spontaneous, not a deliberate arrangement to have sex, and never for a set timeframe.

Oh God, how would I have reacted if Josh had arranged anonymous sex for me as we had discussed? Everything was so confusing right now.

"Come back to bed, Cassie." His husky voice drew me to him.

I slowly padded to the bed. Marcus had propped up several pillows and gestured for me to use them.

"Why?" I asked. I needed some answers before I really lost my mind. "Why are we not having sex right now?"

"Because I'm the one in control." He looked at me. "This weekend is about pleasure. Right now, you're strung so tight, you wouldn't enjoy anything."

"You're the one who caused that." I was perfectly aware I was as taut as a bowstring. My nerves danced, and my muscles twitched.

"I had hoped that dinner would calm you down, not make you tenser."

"I should leave."

"No." The word burst from him as he snagged my wrist.

"This isn't going to work." He didn't understand. I didn't have a clue how I could relax with him. I couldn't give up my control. Not to a dominant man like him. Not to any dominant man. Never again.

"It will." His grip on my wrist loosened, and our gazes clashed. "Relax a bit and realize nothing is going to happen that you don't want to happen."

"Even if I say no to sex?" I didn't understand why he was being so reasonable.

"Sweetheart." Tugging me to him, he cupped my shoulders, his heat sinking into my skin. "I'm not into force. And I don't think *not* having sex is the issue." His cheek touched mine as he leaned close. "You want me as much as I want you."

Might as well acknowledge it. He could read the desire in my anyhow. "Yes," I whispered. I did want him.

"Not while you're afraid."

"I'm not."

"Bullshit." He moved his lips to my earlobe and then bit it gently. I shivered in response.

Chapter Ten

♥

Marcus

I'd sensed her fear from the moment she arrived. I wasn't going to let Cassie out of the deal, but I wouldn't push tonight. This was for her as much as it was for me. I could be patient. "How about a movie?" I shifted away from her tempting body.

Flipping through the channel directory, I found a romantic comedy. Not my usual taste, but maybe it would help Cassie relax. I settled against the pillows. She let out a sigh and arranged her pillows before lying against them.

I kept one eye on her and another on the movie. This woman was tying me up in knots, and damn if I didn't like it. I'd always known she wouldn't be a pushover, but her independence and need for control made me admire her more.

It was more than that too. I'd wanted women before, but never to the extent where I'd made a deal like this one. There was something beneath the surface of Cassie that called to me. Her sensuality shimmered right beneath her skin, if she'd only let it out.

My cock hadn't softened since I'd opened the front door. Every time I touched her, my blood sang with fascination of her soft skin, and my heart pounded with need. Her sexuality needed to be coaxed out of her, and I was the man for the job. Once it was freed, passion would take over. That was, if she would cooperate.

Cassie shifted, and I hid a smile as her gaze drifted over me. I hadn't bothered to pull the cover up, so my dick pushed against my boxers. She wanted to pretend there was nothing between us other than sex, but she was wrong. Lust was the beginning. I wanted more from her than sex—I wanted to know her and for her to know me. Our connection was deeper than sex, and I'd show her the truth by the time our weekend ended.

She was mine.

Chapter Eleven

♥

Cassie

I couldn't concentrate on the movie, and it was one I usually enjoyed. I was too aware of the man next to me on the bed. I peeked at him from beneath my lashes. Damn, he was built. Not a spare ounce of fat on him. A lean torso, sprinkled with dark hair that made my fingers itch to touch. His stomach muscles contracted with each deep breath he took, making my heart flutter.

And his scent... I would never get enough of the pure masculine allure of pine and...

I couldn't put my finger on it, but he smelled deliciously all male. A part of me wanted to throw myself at him while the other part wanted to run in the opposite direction. I wanted to follow the second option because I was afraid of how he made me feel.

With Marcus, I felt soft, feminine, and all woman. He made me think I was more like my mother than I believed. My breath stilled. I wasn't submissive to the point of being a slave. But I wanted Marcus.

Keep it to sex. Leave emotions out of the equation and I could make this work to my advantage. I pushed everything out of my mind except the sound of our breathing, in and out. I shifted closer to him, my body seeking out the comfort of his.

A slightly calloused hand closed over mine. My gaze met his as he raised my hand, and his lips caressed my knuckles. The instant his lips touched my skin, my body turned to jelly. Good thing I was already reclining on the bed or I would've been a puddle on the floor. Liquid heat flowed through my veins. A simple caress from him did this to me.

"I want you," I whispered. No holding back. I'd made up my mind.

The TV went dark. "Lay down on your stomach."

My tummy fluttered, and I reminded myself I could call a stop to this anytime I wanted. Marcus would listen. I did as he said.

"Good girl." His fingers swept my hair to one side. His lips nibbled along the back of my neck, causing shivers to dance up and down my spine. My body was so tuned in to what he was doing.

"I'm going to take this slow." His mouth caressed the nape of my neck. "You smell like the fresh sunshine of the new day. Do you taste the same?" His tongue swept over my skin, and damn if it didn't feel good. The tension began to leave my body.

"You taste like a rich soufflé."

I giggled, and my body grew lax.

"That's better." The bed shifted. I turned my head and glanced at Marcus. His eyes glowed like twin emeralds. "Can I take your nightshirt off?"

I nodded, rolled over, and sat up. He lifted the nightshirt, and I raised my arms over my head as he whisked it off my body. Goosebumps broke out over my skin, and I had to resist the urge to cover my breasts with my hands. Of course my nipples were hard.

"Thank you," he whispered, dropping a soft kiss on my cheek. "Let's have some fun." He opened the nightstand drawer.

I tensed. How many times had I heard the drawer in my parents' bedroom open and shut, then my mother scream in pain? I held my breath, ready to tell Marcus to stop, until I spied the small bottle in his hand.

"Massage oil." He shook the bottle. "Lay back down on your stomach please." I rolled onto my stomach. The mattress moved and he straddled my hips, his cock resting on my fabric-covered ass cheeks.

"You're still too tense. A nice massage will get the kinks out." The *pop* of a lid sounded, then the smell of roses filled the room. He swept his palms over my shoulders. "Knots—and lots of them," he commented.

My eyes fluttered shut as Marcus' magic hands worked on my shoulders. His touch felt sure and firm as he kneaded my muscles. His fingers pressed into my skin, not painfully, but skillfully. I sank deeper into the mattress. His hands were delicious against my skin, finding all those spots that needed attention and some that didn't.

Inch by inch, he massaged my back. My eyes drifted shut as my brain shut down, and I allowed myself to be lulled by the feeling of his hands against my body. If a massage could do this to me, what would sex be like? I couldn't wait.

Chapter Twelve

♥

Marcus

A soft snore made me smile. I didn't stop massaging the oil into Cassie's skin. Her back had been a mess of knots and tension. I lightened my touch and wondered what in her past caused her to be so tight-lipped. Over dinner, she'd talked a little, but her short answers and deflection of my questions made my curiosity rise.

What skeletons were in her closet? Lifting my hands from her luscious skin, I carefully climbed off her hips. She didn't move. All the tension she was carrying had tired her out. Quietly, I put the oil away and washed my hands before returning to bed.

I settled against the pillows. Cassie shifted, mumbled something, then moved toward me. Turning onto my side, I stared at her. Her golden-brown hair was spread out along the pillow; her face turned toward me looked serene in her sleep.

I pulled the sheet up to cover us both. I didn't care if the oil still on her back ruined them. Nothing mattered but Cassie. My cock twitched. I was going to have a long night, but at least I had a view to enjoy. I'd figure out the puzzle Cassie was.

Chapter Thirteen

♥

♥

Cassie

My eyes fluttered open. What time was it? Marcus lay next to me, watching me. "Marcus, what time is it?"

"Hello, sleepyhead." His lips brushed against mine. "It's about two in the morning."

"*Mmm.*" I stretched, and my hand made contact with his crotch. His cock was hard. "I see something else is awake." With boldness I didn't know I possessed, I swept my nails over the fabric-covered head, enticing him through his boxers.

"Witch." This time, he captured my lips and thrust his tongue into my mouth. I toyed with his tongue. I moaned when he cupped my breast, his rough skin tantalizing my softness. He lifted his head.

"More," I whispered. I wanted him.

"Anything my lady wants." Lowering his head, he captured one taut nipple and pulled it into his mouth. My back arched in pleasure as his tongue played with my nipple. Then he switched to the other one.

Need and desire coursed through my veins. His mouth felt like wet heat, making my pussy clench when he sucked my nipples into his mouth. While I'd been asleep, I dreamed of being in Marcus' arms and now... Reality was fantastic.

How could his touch affect me this way? Other lovers left me cold, but not Marcus. I was burning up. My pussy was wet and pulsed with need. He shifted closer to me, his hard cock resting against my leg. His boxers did little to hide his condition.

I slid my hand down in preparation to take his cock in my hand when he trailed kisses from my breasts to my stomach. My hand fell to the side as fire followed his lips, scorching my skin.

"So beautiful," he whispered, guiding me onto my back as his tongue teased my belly button.

Who knew a belly button could be sexy?

When his fingers slipped inside my panties, shivers of excitement fluttered up my spine. Oh, yes. This was what I wanted. His touch, intimately. I lifted my hips as he slid my panties down.

His palms slipped to my inner thighs and pressed outward. I allowed my legs to part. Desire flowed through my veins, leaving a path of wanton destruction. My pussy moistened further.

"Marcus." I breathed out his name.

"Your scent is intoxicating. So fresh, so seductive... I must taste."

His hot breath brushed over my labia, and then his tongue was there, licking from the bottom to the top of my eager slit.

My eyes fluttered shut, only to open when he chuckled. His green eyes blazed with passion and need as he stared at me.

"Tasty." He licked his lips before dropping his head once again. I'd never had a man who seemed to enjoy going down on me.

I arched into his mouth as his tongue swept over my pussy and paused at my clit. My muscles quivered, waiting for him to make his next move.

"Fuck." I breathed out the word as his tongue played with my clit, flicking it from one side to the other, then licking it. My fingers tangled in his raven hair, pulling him closer.

Marcus had a wicked mouth, and he knew how to use it. My stomach tightened, and my pussy throbbed each time he licked me. He shifted and pushed my legs wider. His finger slipped into my cunt. Sweet heaven. Each caress of his finger had my pussy contracting around the hard digit.

It was as if Marcus had awakened a craving inside me, one I hadn't even been aware of. A moan escaped my lips. With each scrape of his finger inside me, my nerves throbbed with more than need, more than want, more than... I didn't know what.

He thrust a second finger inside my pussy and drew my clit into his mouth. Fuck, fuck, fuck. The word repeated over and over in my head. My skin tingled, and my toes curled. I gripped his hair as I cried out. An orgasm rolled over me without me even knowing I was that close. How did that happen? No man had ever made me come from his mouth and fingers. But they hadn't taken their time with me the way Marcus did.

Unknown emotions crashed through me, and I tugged at his head. I needed a minute to recover.

He was grinning when he lifted his head. "Come for me again." A third finger slid inside my hot wetness as he lowered his head.

"No," I whispered. The tension was already building in me. How was this happening? My stomach tightened; my body quivered.

"Fuuuuck," I cried out as my hips arched, pressing me deeper into his mouth when his fingers found my G-spot. A soft scream followed as another orgasm flowed through my body. How was this possible? I rarely had one climax, but two? This man was magic.

"Marcus..." I could only whisper his name as my mind grappled with what just happened. It was all too much. My brain shut down with all the sensations this man caused within me. "Please..."

His gaze was molten when it captured mine. I couldn't look away. His lips shone, wet with my juices. Slowly he gentled his touch and slid his fingers free from me.

"You were fantastic," he said as his lips placed a kiss on my stomach, leaving an imprint.

My body shook with the aftermath of my climaxes. My brain was a scrambled mess. Tears filled my eyes. What the hell had just happened? My breathing was choppy, and I was losing control of my emotions. I didn't want to feel this way. I needed my control, to control my emotions, but I was losing it because he gave me multiple orgasms?

"Did I hurt you?" His voice held concern.

His question caused more tears to flood my eyes. "No...I..." I hiccupped. I needed to get out of this bed. Now. "Let me up, please."

Marcus rolled off of me. I sprang off the bed and high-tailed it into the bathroom as if the hounds of hell were after me, slamming the door shut. They probably were in my mind. How could I allow Marcus to do this? He'd controlled me as surely as my father had controlled my mother. He'd controlled my bodily functions, my heart, my head. Everything. All because of sex.

I leaned against the door, breathing hard, praying Marcus wouldn't follow me. My heart was ready to burst from my chest, and sweat beaded my skin. The bitter taste of fear coated my mouth. I waited, but I didn't hear any sounds from the other side of the door. I pushed myself away and stepped up to the sink to stare at myself in the mirror.

My face was flushed, my eyes wide, and my lips swollen. I had the look of a well-satisfied woman. So why was I in the bathroom instead of in Marcus' arms? Because fear was controlling me. My fingers curled into my palms.

Control. I'd given control to Marcus, and I didn't know how to get it back. Turning on the faucet, I splashed cold water on my face and then examined my features in the mirror. I looked the same, but something fundamental had changed inside me.

My nerves buzzed with excitement and need. I'd never felt this way before. Yes, I'd been with men but rarely climaxed. Marcus had done it without his cock, using only his lips and fingers. I wasn't so sure I liked the fact that he could do that to me so easily.

His touch had been so good, so gentle, and so different from my experiences. I was used to men who were rough, caring little for my pleasure. *You've been with the wrong men,* a voice inside me whispered.

With Marcus, I'd melted at his first touch. My pussy grew wet thinking about it. So why was I still in the bathroom when a man who made my body crave more lay outside the door? Straightening my shoulders, I turned and left the bathroom. Nothing would be settled while I was hiding.

Marcus stood by the bed, fluffing the pillows. Gone were the beige sheets and in their place was a set of gray sheets. He'd changed the bed while he waited for me. He turned and smiled at me. My heart stuttered at his imploring gaze.

"Come back to bed, sweetheart." He held his hand out to me.

My fear of being dominated returned full force. I maneuvered around him and settled on the far side of bed. I stretched out, dangerously close to the edge. I needed distance between us until I could get myself under control.

Who was I kidding? I had never been in control tonight.

The mattress dipped as Marcus climbed onto the bed. He lightly stroked my spine before the lights went off. I stiffened.

"Cassie?"

"I know this is going to sound silly, but do you have a nightlight?" Why hadn't I thought of that before? Even now, as an adult, I couldn't stand total darkness.

"Give me a minute?" His fingers trailed over my back before he climbed out of bed. I rolled onto my back and waited. There was a little light coming from the windows, but not enough to make me feel comfortable.

A match flared. My gaze focused on the flame. "I hope a candle will work?" The wick flared to life, chasing away the ghosts in my imagination. He set it on the nightstand with a dish under it. He sat on the bed.

"That's fine." Gratitude filled me. He didn't think I was being silly. "Thank you."

"Would the bathroom light be better?"

"No." I placed my hand on his forearm when he would have gotten up to turn on the bathroom light. "The candle is fine." It was enough to chase away the shadows.

He nodded, and I removed my hand. Marcus settled into bed and turned to me, his arm curving around my waist as I turned on my side and faced him.

"This isn't going to work, is it?" I whispered.

"It will if we can talk about it. Can you tell me what happened?"

In the semi-darkness, I wanted to share with him, but I wasn't ready yet. "I can't." Maybe in the morning I could, but not now. Not like this.

"Okay." He brushed his finger over my lips. "Go to sleep. Tomorrow is another day." He drew me closer and closed his eyes.

After several minutes, I relaxed, and my breathing evened out. "You're a good man, Marcus DeLuca," I whispered.

He chuckled. "Maybe, but I can also be a very bad boy. Now sleep."

"I happen to like bad boys."

Chapter Fourteen

♥

Cassie

Early the next morning, I slipped from Marcus' hold and out of bed, quietly crossing the room to find my robe. The last thing I wanted to do was wake him, especially as my comment about liking bad boys still echoed through my mind.

It was almost six in the morning, and I couldn't lie in bed anymore. I slipped on my robe and walked to the soft bench seat at the window. Marcus stirred, and my gaze darted to him. When he settled down, I breathed a sigh of relief. My mind was still in turmoil, and I needed time to think.

I needed to be honest with myself. I wanted to be close to him, yet at the same time, run a thousand miles away.

Sitting down, I pulled my knees up, wrapped my arms around them, and stared out the window. My loss of my emotional control last night still bothered me. Not to mention, Marcus brought me to two climaxes with hardly any effort. I needed to find a way to deal with both, because I was afraid it would happen again with him.

Staring out the window, I watched the sky lighten as the sun rose—light yellow gave way to orange, until the sky turned blue. I didn't have a lot of time left to come up with answers. There was no denying I wanted Marcus, or I never would have agreed to the weekend. But now, everything seemed different.

He made me come twice. My tears last night had resulted from part amazement and part fear. The amazement? He'd been able to give me two orgasms without fucking me. The fear...was how he was able to get me to lose my control so easily.

I'd gotten good at faking it with others, but with Marcus, there was no need. He played me like a fiddle and knew exactly how to make me drown in pleasure. I sighed and rested my forehead against the window. I was no closer to answers now than I'd been last night. What was I going to do?

Chapter Fifteen

♥

Marcus

I woke slowly, and my arms were empty. I reached across the bed, but the sheets were cool to my touch. I laid still and listened. No water running, so she wasn't in the shower. Turning my head, I gazed around the room.

The candle was barely giving off any light now, but the sun had come up. There she was. Curled up on the window seat, staring out at the sunrise. A beautiful woman silhouetted by the outside light behind her. I wanted to drink it in, to just watch her.

I glanced at the clock—seven. After giving her two mind-blowing orgasms, we'd gone to sleep around three-thirty. Ready to call her back to me, I noticed her trembling.

Sliding out of bed in my underwear, I pulled the quilt off the bed and joined her. I settled the fabric around her shoulders, tucking it in before sitting near her feet. "How long have you been up?"

"What time is it?"

"Seven." I kept my gaze on her.

"A little over an hour." She snuggled into the quilt. "I don't sleep very well."

"Why not?" At least she was talking to me. I was afraid she'd retreat behind that brick wall of hers. This was a good start.

"Not sure." She shrugged. "The doctors tell me there's nothing wrong, but after about five hours, I wake up, and my mind refuses to shut back down."

"But you only slept about three hours." I wanted to reach out and pull her into my arms, but she looked so closed off that I held back.

"I napped earlier. It really doesn't matter." She shook her head.

"I'll have to see what I can do to wear you out so you'll sleep more." Leaning forward, I brushed my lips over hers.

I fully expected her to push me away, but instead her arms twined around my neck, and the quilt fell from her shoulders. I fought to keep the kiss soft, tracing the seam of her lips with my tongue, feeling their smoothness, but also tasting her undeniable sweetness. I broke the kiss and gazed down at her. "Now *that* was a good morning kiss."

"There are different kinds?" She tilted her head, a glint of amusement overshadowing the melancholy I saw in her eyes, and a small smile played around her lips.

She was joking with me—a very good sign. "You bet there are." I brushed a kiss across her cheek until my lips nibbled at her ear. "I'm going to show you each and every one."

"I can't wait."

My dick jumped, and I forced myself to pull back from her delicious lips and her alluring scent. "Breakfast first and then we'll discuss our day."

Her nose scrunched up, and she made a face at me. I laughed, dropped a kiss on her nose, and stood.

Cassie let out a small gasp, and I looked down to see my boxers had slid down, revealing my hard cock. "Later, he's all yours." Without a backward glance, I grabbed a pair of fresh briefs and running shorts out of the dresser and headed for the bathroom.

After a quick brush of my teeth, a shave, and mastur-bating—necessary if I wanted to give Cassie time to get used to *us* as an us—I felt better. Leaving the bathroom, I found Cassie in the walk-in closet, sorting through her clothes.

"I'm going to start coffee," I said. "Come downstairs when you're ready." Unable to help myself, I brushed another kiss over her lips. "I'd tell you to leave your clothes off, but I want you to be comfortable, so wear whatever you want."

Whistling, I walked out of the room and down the stairs. In the kitchen, I glanced out the window. The sun was shining. It was going to be a very nice, sunny spring day. Maybe later, I could convince Cassie to go skinny dipping in the pool, since it was heated and usable year-round.

After putting the coffee on, I turned to find Cassie standing in the doorway, wearing the teddy I'd sent her earlier in the week. I'd found it in the drawer and left it hanging in the bathroom where she was sure to find it. My dick hardened, and my mouth went dry.

The midnight blue fabric hugged her figure. Her breasts threatened to spill out from the lacy bodice; the fabric was so sheer, I could see her nipples. My gaze traveled over her body, and I swallowed hard. The lace did nothing to hide the outline of her pussy from me, and her legs seemed to go on forever.

"Can I help you get breakfast ready?" Her voice was soft.

Why couldn't I breathe? Without a word, I crossed over to her, tugged her into my arms, and covered her lips with mine.

The minty toothpaste she used burst upon my taste buds as our tongues dueled for dominance. My tongue retreated, and hers followed. Cassie deepened the kiss, and I let her, my arms tightening around her.

Passion. She vibrated with it, was on fire with it, and I wanted to stoke the flames until they were out of control, but at the same time, I knew I needed some answers.

Her fear appeared to be muted this morning, since she wasn't shying away from me as she had last night. My hands moved over her semi-bare back to her ass. I cupped those luscious ass cheeks in my palms as I pressed my hips to hers.

I broke the kiss, and my lips trailed across her cheek, to her ear. "What's changed?"

She tensed for a second then relaxed back into my embrace. "I don't know what you mean."

Squeezing her ass, I rotated my hips, letting her feel my hard cock. I leaned back to stare into her eyes. "Last night you were nervous and so wound up that I was afraid you'd snap like a dry twig."

"It had been a stressful day, and I didn't know what to expect."

"And today you do?" I didn't think I was that predictable.

"Well…" As she shifted, my cock rubbed against her pussy through the fabric. "You took care of me last night without any expectations. Plus I've known you want me."

I nodded. Of course, I wanted her. I hadn't made a secret of that.

"And I want you."

That was obvious, since she was here in my home. If she didn't want me, she wouldn't be here. I waited, watching her face for any signs of distress or fear, but I didn't see any. "Fear doesn't disappear overnight."

Her blue eyes widened. "It wasn't fear of you."

"Wasn't it?" I needed to know about her fear.

She licked her lips, and I fought my own urges to swoop down and take her rosy mouth in a deep hard kiss.

"I needed some time to deal with what I was feeling, what you made me feel." Her gaze skittered away before returning. "I rarely climax with a man, let alone have multiple orgasms."

I barely prevented my mouth from dropping open. I shook my head. "You've been with the wrong men." That was the only explanation.

"Apparently."

Taking a deep breath, I loosened my hold on her. "You put the teddy on to make a statement." I liked how relaxed and playful she was this morning, and I wanted to keep her that way. But I wanted to make sure her fear didn't overwhelm her either.

"Yes. I found it hanging behind the door this morning. Otherwise, I'd have worn it last night." She gripped my shoulders. "I want this weekend with you."

"Good. I want it too." I truly believed what she said. Cassie was a strong woman. She'd have told me to go to hell.

"You're right. I would have told you to go to hell, probably should have," she said.

Had I spoken the words out loud? Apparently so.

I hid my surprise at her admission. Would I ever get to the real Cassie? I suspected I was seeing her now, at least, a small part of what lay behind the curtain she used like a shield. Her stomach growled. I laughed and forced myself to release her.

"I better feed you breakfast, then we can play." Moving to the fridge, I pulled out ham, eggs, and cheese before looking over my shoulder at her. "If you want to help, you can chop the ham while I get the eggs ready."

"You got it." She smiled, and the whole room lit up.

We worked together in silence, and I found I liked having her here. A first for me. I usually hated having anyone else in my kitchen, but with Cassie, it was different. She didn't try to carry on a conversation or get in my way. It was as if we were in total sync with each other, no matter who was doing what.

I slid the finished omelets onto the plates and carried them to the breakfast bar while Cassie refilled our coffee cups. She slid onto the stool and picked up her fork, cut a piece, and lifted it to her mouth. "*Mmmm*." She hummed as she swallowed. "That's good. Talk about melt in your mouth."

"I have other delicacies that will melt in your mouth." Lord, this woman turned me on with her pleasure at eating good food.

"Oh." She peeked at me from beneath her lashes, and the heat from her gaze made my dick stiffen.

"Yep." I grinned. It had been a long time since I'd had a lover I could have fun with. I'd been right to follow my gut about Cassie.

Silence fell as we ate, and when she was done, she slipped from the stool and carried her plate and cup to the sink. I followed, and when she turned, it was right into my arms. I pressed her ass against the sink.

"I want you to be yourself this weekend."

"Huh?" She tilted her head and confusion made her wrinkle her nose. So cute.

"I told you last night this weekend is about pleasure." I took her in my arms and trailed my fingers trailed up her spine, tunneling under her hair, my nails tracing the nape of her neck. "Pleasure can be fun."

"I'm sure it can be."

"It will be." I lowered my forehead to hers. "What is your middle name?"

"Michelle. Why?"

"If I do anything you don't want me to do, or if you start feeling uncomfortable at all, I want you to say *Michelle*, and I'll stop. That's your safe word."

"Will you stop?"

Her breathless question hit me in the stomach like a sucker punch. Shit, had some man not stopped when she told him to? Had that man hurt her so bad that she was still struggling with it? Was that why she hid her sensuality? So many questions and no answers.

"Yes, I will stop, no matter what we're doing. You have my word on it, Cassie."

I didn't know what else I could say to reassure her I would stop. Because I would. I meant what I said, and maybe it was time to show her.

"Why don't we take this upstairs to the bedroom?" Taking her hand, I guided her out of the kitchen and up the curved staircase. When we entered the room, Cassie tugged her hand away, hurried to the bed, and started making it.

"You don't need to do that." I lounged against the wall, watching the way her pert ass wiggled as she bent over, tucking in the sheet. How the teddy she wore shifted up. My dick reacted; I liked the view. Cassie flittered around, straightening the sheets and covers. What was going through her head? We were just going to mess the bed up again.

Chapter Sixteen

♥

Cassie

"Yes, I do." *Beds must always be made—your father hates messy beds.* My mother's words echoed in my head. Why did this keep happening?

"We're only going to mess it up again."

"I know, but..." I stopped and the quilt slipped from my fingers. I glanced at Marcus, confusion sweeping through me. "I don't know how to do this." Did that even make sense?

He pushed away from the wall and crossed to me. Taking my hands, he kissed the back of them. Tingles from the touch of his lips against my skin swept over me. "Do what feels good, and let me take care of you."

That sounded so nice. No one had ever really taken care of me. Could I release that little bit of control to Marcus? For the rest of our time together, let him take the lead and take care of me? I was going to try. "Yes." The whispered word left my lips.

"Come on." He swept me into his arms, and I let out a small squeal as he carried me into the bathroom. "First things first," he said setting me on my feet. "While I adore this on you..." His fingers found the ties holding the teddy together. "I want you naked." He pulled the ties, and the fabric slipped away. "You are so beautiful."

"I..." I couldn't find the words. His look was... I didn't know how to describe it. It was something like worship.

He brushed his fingers over my breasts. "Rosy, perky nipples. I plan on playing with these a lot this weekend." He pinched them lightly, and my knees went weak. He slid open the shower door and turned on the water.

With a quick motion, he slid his shorts and underwear off, kicking them to the side. I couldn't help myself. I gazed down at him. His cock was hard. I closed my eyes and bit my lip. Was I nervous? Scared? Aroused? Maybe all three.

"You're...well-endowed." Those were lame words, but they were the only ones that came to mind. He stifled a laugh, then said, "Let's get wet."

Too late.

Snagging me around the waist, he maneuvered us into the shower and closed the door.

The shower was huge. It would easily hold four people, but it was more than that. There was water all around us. Last night I'd only used the main shower head, but now I was surrounded by all the water jets.

The water pulsed around my upper back and stomach. Even lower around my legs. It was decadent, erotic. Marcus nudged me farther under the spray, and I ducked my head, allowing the hot water to flow over me.

His lips touched the back of my neck in a soft kiss. His chest was against my back, and I allowed my head to fall back against his shoulder. Heat surrounded me, not just from the water. Every nerve ending came alive with this man.

"You smell delicious." His lips trailed over my shoulder, skimming over my skin, leaving fire in its path.

I sucked in a breath when something cold and smooth touched me below my breasts. Lifting my head off his shoulder I glanced down. "What the heck is that?" I was more curious than alarmed. The beige, cock-shaped soap was about four inches long, and I almost wanted to laugh when I figured out what it was.

"This is just a little something I've been working on in R&D."

"Oh?"

"Yes." He let the soap drop from his fingers but held on to it with a rope embedded at one end. "Cock on a rope."

"Oh my God."

"Women in our focus groups have told us they want to have fun in the shower when they don't have a man around to please them. Some complain that waterproof vibrators don't always do the trick."

"You mentioned in the staff meeting you were working on products from the last focus group, but I didn't realize any of them were ready. I receive a lot of calls and emails asking when we will have new products out."

"The women in the focus group were very forthcoming and seemed to like this."

He pulled me closer as he held the soap under the water and lathered up his hands. "This soap has many uses." He slid the rope onto a hook and then his palms covered my breasts.

A moan slipped past my lips as he lathered my breasts, paying careful attention to my nipples. The scent of vanilla wafted up with each pass of his palms over my tits. My nipples were hard when he circled them with his fingers.

"I hope you like the vanilla scent. I wanted to find something that smelled nice, but also pleased women."

He lifted the hand-held shower head and directed the spray over my chest, washing away the soap. My nipples ached, and I wanted his hands on them again. I shifted from one foot to the other.

"Of course," he continued, "the model on the wall is our standard version."

"Standard?" Was that my breathless voice? Of course it was. This man did that to me. Marcus made me so hot and needy I was surprised the water didn't sizzle as it hit my skin. Each time his fingers brushed over me, my pussy clenched with desire.

"Yes." He tilted his head back, his eyes glinting with wickedness, and I shivered with a delicious sliver of anticipation.

"Do you trust me?"

My heart pounded, but I nodded. I did trust him.

He took my lips in a deep, hard kiss, causing my knees to weaken. His arm curved around my waist before they gave out.

"You'll be the first person outside of my R&D team to try out newest item." Again, something smooth and cool touched my stomach, and I started to look down.

"No, sweetheart." His teeth closed over my earlobe, and my gut clenched. "No peeking. Close your eyes and just feel."

I took a shaky breath and willed myself to settle down and rest against him. It wasn't easy; my body was on high alert.

"That's it, baby," he whispered as he slipped his hand lower. "Spread your legs for me."

I shifted my feet, anticipation heating my blood. He was going to soap me down there? It wasn't like I hadn't done that before, but... This was different. This was foreplay in a shower, something I'd never done and certainly not with a man like Marcus.

He rubbed the soap up and down, but there was something different about this one. I couldn't put my finger on it. A gasp left my lips as his fingers spread my labia and ran the soap over my clit.

"Remember when I said the women wanted something to please them?"

My mind turned the words over in my head as he guided the soap over my clit. My pussy clenched with each pass. Greedy little thing.

"Spread your legs wider."

I shifted my feet farther apart until cool air teased me. I lost my breath when he paused the soap at my entrance. Pure pleasure swept through me as he pressed the soap into my pussy.

"*Ahh!*" My mouth dropped open. "It's bigger." That was the difference. Hell, yes.

"Yes, this is a larger version. Women complained the waterproof vibrator wasn't big enough, and the larger ones became awkward."

The soap slipped farther into my channel, and my muscles clenched around it. That didn't stop Marcus from continuing to stroke me with it.

"The soap is hypo-allergenic. Our focus group gave us the dimensions they felt would be best for most women." The soap-cock slipped out, and Marcus pushed it back in. "The rope is made to go over your wrist and tighten so you won't lose it."

Lose it? My pussy was clenching the thing like it was a real cock. It wasn't going to get lost. My hips arched when he brushed his thumb over my clit. Oh damn, that upped my arousal.

"We've been thinking in R&D about adding something to the soap so a woman can tease her clit at the same time."

His finger, slick with soap, found my clit and flicked it.

"I think what you have is more than enough." I don't know how I managed to say the words with the way Marcus was stroking my pussy and clit.

My nerves tingled, and my pussy clenched. My eyes drifted shut as he continued to fuck me with the cock on a rope. My body was twitching with need. "More," I whispered, arching my hips. He adjusted his hold and twisted the cock. I jerked.

"Easy, sweetheart."

He pulled the soap from me, and I groaned in disappointment. I was so close. His fingers were spreading my pussy lips apart and... "*Ahhh.*"

Warm water hit my pussy and clit. I shifted away from the spray. It was too much.

"Just removing all the lather." He maneuvered the spray, and the pulsing water cascaded over my clit, sending me right back to the edge.

A single touch or a finger in my pussy and I'd go over. The water disappeared, and I cried out when he plunged two fingers into my cunt.

"Yes!" I bucked into his touch.

"You're so slick, so warm and tight."

My hips followed the rhythm of his fingers as my pussy pulsed, and my stomach quivered with my impending orgasm. I was almost there.

His fingers were gone.

"Damn it, stop teasing me." I opened my eyes and glared at him.

"The wait will be worth it." He gave me a smug grin.

"Really." An idea popped into my head. He wanted to play the teasing game. Well, let's see how he liked it.

I bit my lower lip so I wouldn't grin and give my plan away. I maneuvered in his loose hold until I faced him. Without a word, I dropped to my knees and drew his rock-hard cock into my mouth.

"Cassie," he groaned.

I traced the veins of his cock with my fingertips then grasped the base before I took the crest between my lips and caressed the tiny slit with the tip of my tongue.

Steel covered by silk.

"Fuck." His hips shifted, and his hands tangled in my wet hair.

Phase two, I thought, very glad now I had the foresight to read several sex manuals made available to company employees. I drew him deep into my mouth, and my fingers slid to his balls, which I caressed while my mouth and tongue teased his cock.

His hips thrust as his cock slid in and out of my mouth. Pleasure flooded me—I was getting to him. Relaxing my throat, I took him all the way back. Deeper than I'd ever taken a man. His balls tightened in my grasp. I drew back and released his cock, a grin playing around my lips.

"Cassie," he groaned, his fingers caressing the back of my head.

"The wait will be worth it." I mimicked his words.

His fingers tightened as I rose, then slid over my back to cup my ass. His eyes were blazing with desire. "Who's teasing who?"

Tilting my head, I gave him a saucy grin. "Turnabout is fair play."

"Then by all means, let's play." He pulled me to him, and his lips descended.

The kiss was one of passion and possession. I sank against his body and kissed him back. My skin was on fire for him. I needed him. I'd never needed a man like this before.

The water stopped flowing, and Marcus maneuvered us out of the shower while we still kissed. Once we were clear of the shower, he lifted me into his arms and carried me to the bed.

Harder, deeper, our tongues dueled as we groaned into each other's mouths. He broke the kiss when my feet touched the carpeted floor. I watched him as he threw the covers back, enjoying the way the muscles on his back moved and contracted.

"We'll get the sheets wet."

"Who cares?" He lifted me and tossed me onto the bed, following me down.

His legs trapped mine, and he grabbed my wrists, pulling my arms above my head. His weight felt so good. In the past, I'd hated being enclosed like this by lovers, feeling trapped. Not with Marcus.

"Mine," he whispered before lowering his head. His tongue licked my puckered nipple. My breath rushed out at the pure pleasure of his tongue against my skin. He flashed me a smirk before he closed his lips over my right nipple and his hand over my left. Molten lava flowed through my veins. He'd worked me up earlier, and my body was primed and ready.

"More." Yes, I wanted more. I wanted everything he would give me and then some.

"My pleasure." He stretched his arm out, reaching for the nightstand drawer.

"I'm on the pill." I wanted to feel him, not a condom.

"Good, but a condom is not what I'm after."

Chapter Seventeen

♥

C assie

I stiffened as Marcus slid the drawer open—I couldn't help it. Was he reaching for something to hurt me with? Was he more like my father than I thought? My memories of hearing the bedside drawer open, followed by my mother screaming, filled my head.

Or did Marcus have something much more dangerous? How many times could he hit me before I said my safe word? And would he stop?

"Michelle." The word rushed out along with what little breath I had.

He froze, and his gaze caught mine.

"Sweetheart?" He dropped to my side, his arm encircling my waist, cradling me against him. His touch was comforting.

Oh God, I was acting like a frightened virgin. I opened my mouth, but I couldn't find the words to demand he release me.

"Did I scare you?" His voice was soft as his hands stroked up and down my back, soothing me.

"It's not you." A tremor shook me. In my heart, Marcus wasn't the issue. I knew that. But unpleasant memories kept interfering, and I didn't have a clue how to stop them.

Fear lurked in my mind, no matter how much my body craved Marcus' touch. If only I could get past my fears. That way, if I knew what he was reaching for, maybe I could handle it better and wouldn't panic. I needed to find a way to trust Marcus, or we'd never get anywhere.

I decided to test that theory. "What were you searching for?"

"A toy." He shifted, reached into the drawer, and settled next to me. "This is another new invention we've come up with in R&D." He held up the small toy for me to see.

It was shaped oddly with something like two suction cups on the end of it. I tilted my head one way then the other as my fear receded. "What is it?" Curiosity was getting the better of me.

"May I show you?"

"Will it hurt?"

"No. It's made to bring pleasure, not pain."

My fingers shook as I reached out to touch the gadget in his palm. "They're suction cups."

"Yes."

I took a deep breath and let it out, my gaze capturing his. "Show me." I had to try to trust him sometime, right? I'm not sure where this braveness came from, but the way his eyes lit up made my heart soar.

"Only if you're sure."

Always giving me an out. He'd stopped when I said my safe word. Maybe I could trust him. Keep trying was all I could tell myself. "I can't guarantee I'll always be sure, but if you say this is for pleasure, I'm sure."

"Lie on your back."

I did as he said and watched him. I reached up to trace the lines on his forehead. "I'll be okay. I needed to see what you were getting. The unknown sometimes frightens me." Pain frightens me. Loss of control frightens me. Would I ever get over these fears?

He nodded. "One day you will tell me why, but for right now, I'm going to play with your breasts and nipples." My hand dropped as he lowered his head, and his mouth closed over my right nipple. Tiny shivers went through my body as he licked and sucked until the nipple was rock hard, then he did the same with the left.

By the time he was done, flames engulfed my entire being. I kept my gaze on his hand when he placed the small suction cups over my nipples.

"I want you to talk to me about how this feels. Tell me about the pleasure you feel. Tell me what else you want me to do."

It took a minute for his words to penetrate the sensual haze over my brain. He was giving me control.

My heart swelled. This dominant man was gifting me control. I almost couldn't believe it. Then he tapped the remote in his hand, and my mouth dropped open.

"Goodness." My hands rose to cover my breasts, but he intercepted them.

"No touching, sweetheart. Talk to me about what you feel?"

My chest shuddered as I took a deep breath. "The cups are sucking my nipples, and it's so good."

"Better than a man's mouth?"

I scrunched up my nose as I pondered his question. "Yes and no. The suction is strong, but not as warm."

"I'll make note of that. Ready for the next step?"

"Yes." This was fun. I couldn't wait to see what came next.

He touched the remote again. My lips opened with a gasp. Pleasure flew through my body as the sucking continued, but now it felt like someone was licking the tip of my nipples. They were so hard and sensitive. "You are a wicked man."

He laughed. One of his deep husky laughs I felt in my bones and made me want to hear it again and again. "What does it feel like?"

"Something like a tongue is licking the tip of my nipples, while the suction continues."

"It's working as it should. Any pain?"

"No." Pleasure. My pussy was getting wet, and my skin flushed with need.

"Good. I'm going to move on." He placed his palms on my thighs and spread my lax legs apart. "I've been dying to taste you again."

"Marcus." I cried out when he licked my pussy. With his palms on my hips, he lifted his head and stared at me.

"Talk to me, sweetheart. Let me know I'm not scaring you." He dropped his head and found my clit.

"You're not." I panted, squirming on the sheets. "I'm burning up, and you're stoking the fire by licking and—" I cried out, my hips arching off the mattress as he slipped two fingers into my wet core.

Oh yes. My fingers curled into my palms as rivers of pleasure ran riot through me. It started at my pussy and traveled to my breasts, then back again. With each pass of his tongue against my clit, each stroke of his fingers in my pussy, with each movement of his toy, my pleasure ratcheted up, but it wasn't enough.

"I need more." My voice was raspy, my fingers sliding over his head to tangle in his hair. Touching him made the connection between us more prominent.

He curved his fingers, hitting my G-spot, and I exploded. My back bowed as he drew my clit into his mouth. I opened my mouth, trying to suck in air. I couldn't breathe or think. The pleasure swept through every part of me. Pure, unadulterated pleasure. I finally collapsed against the mattress, my eyes closing.

I could only lay there, breathing hard, waiting for my pussy to stop clenching, my skin to stop humming. Yes, I wanted more. I wanted to feel Marcus' cock deep inside me, thrusting in and out of me, taking me to new heights.

"Cassie?" His voice was soft.

"I want you inside me. I want to feel your strength, your passion; I want you." I let the words flow from my lips. I wasn't going to take them back, and I wasn't going to be embarrassed by them.

My lashes fluttered when his fingers touched the toy on my breasts. He turned off and gently removed the suction cups. I inhaled as the cool air hit my nipples and the feeling of... I didn't know how to explain it. It was more than pleasure and need.

"I want you inside me," I whispered as I draped my arms around his neck while he positioned himself over me. He groaned as he sank his cock into me. My hips rose to meet his, and I moaned.

He froze. "Did I hurt you?"

"Hell, no." Our gazes connected. "You feel so good, so big, so manly. I want more."

He grinned, then kissed me softly and pressed forward.

My pussy adjusted to him. While Marcus took his time letting my body get used to his size, I was primed and ready for all of him.

"More. Give me more. Give me all of you."

My nails dug into his skin with each stroke. My hips wouldn't stay still. He nuzzled my neck as he lifted his hips until just the tip of his cock rested inside me, then he sank into my pussy.

"Fuck, yes." He continued at his own pace. He was going to kill me slowly with pleasure; I was sure of it.

"If you don't start moving fast, I'm going to lose my mind. I thought you were going to fuck me?"

He had the nerve to grin. I'd never been this bold or frank with anyone. Marcus was different. He allowed a side of myself to come out that I'd kept hidden for a reason, but now those reasons didn't seem so important.

"I am fucking you *my way*." His mouth was on my throat. I arched my neck, giving him more access, to encourage his touch.

"You're teasing me." My breath caught when he was fully seated in me. My pussy clenched around his hard length, and my tummy fluttered with need.

He groaned when I tightened my pussy around his cock. But he still didn't move. I wasn't sure who was in control here, but it was time to take some action.

"Come on, a turtle moves faster than you do." Taunting him might not be the best idea, but if it got him moving, it would be worth it. "Hell, a vibrator would do a better job than you're doing."

"Really?" He lifted his head. His eyes glowed. "Challenge accepted." He pulled back and sank into me at the same slow pace.

It was all I could do not to pound my fists against his back and demand he go faster. He said challenge accepted, but he still moved way too slow.

"Let go of your control."

"No." I tried to buck against him, but he held my hips immobile with his. "You're an ass, you know that."

"*Hmmm*, don't give me ideas. Have you ever been fucked in the ass?"

Oh. Dear. God. Liquid heat flowed through my veins. I'd never been touched back there. But now, there was no fear, only anticipation and need.

"Not today," he added. "We'll work up to that."

I opened my mouth but lost my breath as he thrust into me, sinking in even farther. God, his cock scraped all my nerve endings and made my body sing out with delight.

"Do you know how much I'm enjoying fucking you?" His breath was hot against my skin. "Maybe later, when you've rested a bit, we'll try it doggy style so I can get deeper."

Deeper? How much farther could he get? I was filled to the brim. He rotated his hips, and a moan slipped from my lips.

"Can you feel me, sweetheart?"

"Every amazing fucking inch."

"Good." His lips caressed my ear. "Get used to my cock sliding into your pussy, because I can keep up this pace for hours."

Hours? My pussy contracted, but his lazy strokes weren't enough to send me over the edge. Yes, I was on the edge, and it wouldn't take a lot to push me over. And damn it, I wanted to go over, taking him with me.

I was going to be a basket case before he was through with me. Could I beat him at his own game? Maybe I could figure it out. He was so hard; he had to be close.

"Fuck me."

His green gaze captured mine. "Tell me what you want?"

"You." The word flowed out, and it was the truth. I wanted Marcus more than anything. He'd done this to me.

He grinned. "Hold on."

He pulled back and slammed back in, then did it again. Faster and harder.

"Yes!" I cried out. This was what I wanted, what I needed. My pussy tightened with each hard thrust. My hips rose to meet his. My fingers grazed down his back as I curled my legs around his ass. "More."

Our harsh breathing filled the room. His fingers trailed over my tummy, moving south.

Yes, yes, YES! I chanted silently.

He brushed my clit, and I cried out. Pleasure and pain collided. I'd been on the brink for so long.

He flicked my clit again, and that was it. My climax crashed over me. My body bowed against his; my pussy convulsed around his hard cock.

"That's it, baby, come for me."

I did. Before my orgasm subsided, another one hit. Marcus didn't miss a beat—he kept thrusting as his fingers played with my sensitive clit.

My entire being hummed, but another climax was already spreading. My toes tingled as he tormented me. He had to be close.

Marcus pulled out and then slammed back in, at the same time pressing down on my clit. My scream, as I arched into him, bounced off the bedroom walls. I could feel him pulsing inside my pussy, spilling his seed. Our bodies undulated against each other, skin scraping skin, until we finally collapsed.

I pried my fingers from his sweaty back and ran them through his hair. "That was incredible."

"It was fantastic." His lips found mine, and he kissed me deeply before rolling onto his back.

I missed his weight, but I laid there, waiting for my heart to return to normal and realized it probably never would. Not around Marcus. He'd already shown me more pleasure than I'd ever known.

He'd opened a side of me that I'd kept hidden, afraid to explore. Good or bad, I'd let that side of myself out tonight. It hadn't been a conscious decision, but now that it had happened, I wasn't sorry. I would see where this led and deal with the consequences later. Turning my head, I stared at him.

His eyes were closed, his face relaxed. My gaze traveled down over his broad chest covered with fine, dark hair, his brown nipples barely visible, to his flat abdomen, to his groin. His cock, for the moment, laid lax against his leg. Damn, even soft he looked big. His cock twitched.

"If you keep staring at me that way, you're going to end up with me buried to the hilt in your pussy sooner than you think."

"And that's a bad thing?" Our gazes met as my fingers traced his taut stomach.

"Witch." He captured my wandering fingers before they reached his groin. "I think it's time we moved to phase two."

"Phase two?" What did this man have in store for me now? Excitement zinged over my skin. I could handle anything he could dish out. At least, I thought I could.

"Yes." He slid off the mattress, and I couldn't help but admire his tight ass as he walked across the room. I licked my lips.

Chapter Eighteen

♥

Marcus

I was aware of Cassie's eyes on me as I crossed to the dresser. I opened the third drawer and pulled out some of the toys I'd hidden there earlier. I put them on the nightstand before walking into the bathroom so she'd have a chance to look the toys over. She didn't do well with surprises. That was something I planned to find out more about but not until Cassie was ready.

Cleaning myself up, I held a fresh washcloth beneath warm water, then grabbed a dry towel. In the bedroom, Cassie sat on the edge of the bed, staring at the items on the nightstand.

"Lay back down, sweetheart." I kept my voice soft.

Her gaze darted to me, then back to the nightstand, before she let out a breath and laid down.

She was tense again. I bit back a sigh. One step forward, five back. Sitting at her hip, I took the warm washcloth and ran it over her face, wiping away the drying perspiration.

Her eyes drifted shut. "That feels good."

"That's the point." I washed her face, neck, arms, and breasts. "Spread your legs, please." I noted her pussy was rosy and kept my touch light as I cleaned her up. The cloth rubbed her clit, and she let out a gasp.

"Sore?" I wouldn't be surprised if she were, since we'd played hard and long tonight.

"Sensitive." Her hips wiggled, but as much as I wanted to, I didn't take the invitation. I finished cleaning her legs, then used the towel to dry her off.

When I finished, I stood and put the washcloth and towel in the hamper. Cassie still lay on her back with her eyes closed. I didn't want to disturb her, but we needed to talk.

"Why did you fight against this for so long?" I asked, sliding back onto the mattress and nudging her over.

"I don't understand your question."

She started to turn away from me, but I gathered her into my arms.

"Don't hide anymore, Cassie. Please."

A sigh left her lips. "I didn't think it was a good idea for us to become involved."

"And?" She'd held something back. I wanted her to stay relaxed, but we needed to talk. I was going to do my best to keep her calm and mellow. I didn't want this conversation to wait too long because Cassie was too good at going on the offense and hiding her true feelings.

When she stayed silent, I cupped her chin and tilted her head up. "Please, look at me, sweetheart."

Our gazes met, and hers was filled with apprehension. "Tell me why?" I asked.

Her tongue moistened her lips. "Because other men have always found me lacking."

"Idiots." I moved my palm to cup her cheek. How could the men in her past think she was lacking? She was perfect, but I saw how it affected her. "*They* were inadequate, not you. Never you."

"But they said—"

My fingers covered her lips, stopping her words. "Shall I prove it to you?"

"Prove what?" she mumbled against my skin.

"That you are a very sexual being and never lacked anything." I removed my hand from her mouth.

Doubt filled her eyes, and I vowed if nothing else came out of this weekend, she would understand her own sensuality better.

"Let's not go off course for the weekend," she said.

"I'm not." I took her mouth in a slow, long kiss, tasting her and enjoying the way she responded to me. The men in her past were damn fools for not being able to see Cassie's pure, raw sensuality, and I was going to tap into that. I wasn't afraid of her passion or her pleasure. I broke the kiss and stared at her.

"I'm going to pleasure you, Cassie. All weekend long. Give yourself over to me." I spoke the words from my heart. I was determined to show her she was a sensual woman.

"I'm not—" Uncertainty crept into her voice.

"You saw the toys I set on the nightstand."

She nodded.

"When you're ready, I'm going to use the egg on you." I loved using that toy on women and seeing the pleasure on their faces.

"Ready? Hell, my pussy is already dripping."

I laughed as I sat up and put some space between us, grabbing three pillows to pile up on the mattress. "I want you to lay on your stomach over these pillows."

She eyed me, then the pillows, before her gaze returned to me.

There wasn't fear there, but uncertainty. "If it bothers you, you know how to stop me." I wanted to remind her

I would quit if she said her safe word. It was something I would always do.

"I want to try." She rolled onto the pillows and positioned herself.

I ran my palms over her ass, and she jumped. "You've got one hell of a sexy ass." I couldn't wait until I could fuck her there. But not today, not for a while. I would have to gain her complete and total trust first.

"Oh, really?" She wiggled her butt at me, and I smiled. I loved it when she was flirty. That was also a good sign. I already knew that when she got cheeky, she'd set aside whatever misgivings she had, at least for the moment. I loved learning about her and planned to have the opportunity to do so for a long, long time.

"Yes, but I like other parts of you as well." I ran two fingers over her crack to her wet pussy. She let out a contented sigh when I pushed them into her, stroking her. "Bring your knees up, sweetheart."

I waited until she got her knees into position. "Spread them apart." Her body wiggled as she shifted. It opened her up to my fingers and my gaze. I swallowed. This woman took my breath away.

I stroked her pussy a few more times, then pulled my fingers away and picked up the egg. "I've got the egg in my hand." Her head was turned away from the nightstand, and I wanted her to know what I was doing.

"And what do you plan on doing with it?"

Her question surprised me. Up until now, she'd not questioned anything I did. Not really. "I'm going to pleasure you with it." Using my fingers, I spread her pussy lips apart and placed the egg at her opening.

With gentle pressure, I pressed it up and into her cunt. She wiggled as I adjusted it the way I wanted it.

"Okay?" I removed my fingers, loving the way her pussy enveloped the egg.

"Yes." Her voice was soft and full of wonder.

Was it possible she'd never played with toys before? How could that be? I shook my head. It didn't make sense. She worked for a sexual fantasy company. Maybe none of her other lovers ever played with her before, never revved her up. Never took the time to find out how Cassie ticked.

I wanted to enjoy her pleasure. My own pleasure came from watching her. The micro expressions on her face as I brought her to completion, her soft sighs at my touch, and the moans from my kisses made me rock hard. Leaning back, I picked up the small remote and turned it on.

"*Ohhhh.*" Her hips pressed down on the pillows. Her skin flushed an enticing shade of pink.

"Like it?" I asked.

"It's different."

"You haven't tried a vibrating egg before?"

"No."

My eyes widened. "A vibrator?" Maybe my assumptions were wrong.

"Yes, I've used a vibrator, but I don't like them."

"Why not?" The question slipped out as my palms covered her pale globes, caressing them.

"Too plastic."

"A common complaint." Goose pimples decorated her skin as I traced the pads of my fingers over her ass, up her spine, and back again. "Tell me what else you've tried?"

She turned her face away from me as her cheeks turned bright red.

"Cassie?"

"This is embarrassing." Her voice was muffled.

"Honey, there is nothing you can't talk to me about. You won't surprise or scare me." I paused. What would put her at ease?

"Why don't I go first?" I suggested. I checked the egg to make sure it was still secure before I slipped my hand between her legs. Yes, it was still in place. "Do you know why I went to work for Fantasies, Inc.?"

"No." Her words were clearer.

"I wanted to create toys to satisfy all sexes, but also because I wanted to see the toys used. I enjoy watching people as they find sexual heaven."

"You're a voyeur?"

The surprise in her voice made me grin. "Sometimes." I turned the egg up a notch, noting the way her hips shifted. "I like to see my toys bring pleasure. Interestingly enough, pleasuring a man through the use of toys can be more difficult than with a woman.

I slipped my fingers down, gathered her moisture, and began massaging her with it.

"What did you create to pleasure a man?"

She was curious and aroused, and my own pleasure grew. "I developed a sleeve a man can put over his cock and an egg to make it vibrate. The thing is, I added two other cylinders to it."

"What do they do?" She was not turning her head from side to side anymore as the egg did its job in her pussy.

I leaned down and blew a breath against her pussy. A gasp left her lips. I settled back on my knees and continued to caress her outer lips and her ass.

"The man puts the sleeve over his cock, then places one cylinder in front of his balls and the other behind until they lock into place."

"Ouch! That sounds like it might hurt." Her breathing sounded choppy.

"Not when it's done right." I removed my fingers from her outer lips. I wanted to do more to her, to bring her pleasure to the boiling point until it spilled over. "Can you roll onto your back and keep the pillows under your hips?"

"I think so." I kneeled next to her and helped her reposition. Her legs lay open, and my mouth watered at the thought of tasting her again.

Soon, I promised myself. First, I had a to finish my explanation.

"The cylinders are something like the egg you have inside your pussy." I flicked the remote up another notch. Her hips shifted. I settled myself between her spread legs. "They stimulate a man's balls, and the sleeve suctions his cock. But he has the controls, so he can find the level he wants."

The egg had started to emerge. Using my finger, I pushed it back into her channel and was rewarded with groan. Placing my palms on her hips, I lowered my head.

I found her clit and flicked it with my tongue before I drew it deep into my mouth. She was dripping and tasted like sweet cotton candy—a taste I was becoming addicted to. Her inner muscles tightened and released. My cock pulsed with need, but I'd deal with that later. This was all for Cassie.

I pressed my tongue against her clit and turned up the vibrations of the toy in her pussy.

A cry left her lips as her body convulsed. I found the remote and turned it up to the highest setting before I continued to feast on her as she came over and over again.

Chapter Nineteen

♥

Cassie

What the hell was Marcus doing to me? I opened my mouth, trying to get more air into my lungs, but between his mouth and the egg, I could barely breathe. My hips arched, the heat in my belly flaring to my thighs and spreading to my toes as another climax rolled over me. I barely got through the first one when another one hit.

Only with Marcus could I have multiple orgasms. I expected him to pull back.

Instead, the egg vibrations seemed to increase. How high did the damn toy go? Did he have any idea what he was doing to me? All these delicious and totally wicked things.

His tongue pressed against my clit as another climax rushed through me, and my body shook. I couldn't control myself. My head thrashed from side to side, and my fingers curled into the sheet. Pleasure. So much plea-sure. Pleasure I never even knew existed. I'd never felt so alive, so much a woman. Damned if I wasn't enjoying everything he was doing to me.

My belly and pussy tightened. Was this orgasm number four or five? I couldn't remember, and I wasn't sure my body could take anymore. "Marcus," I called. Did he even realize what he was doing to me?

"Go with it, sweetheart."

"I can't."

"You can. Give me one more."

He knew what he was doing to me and wasn't about to stop unless I said my safe word. I wasn't going to say it. His mouth was now on my pussy as the egg vibrated harder. Didn't he understand? My pussy was already nothing but a big bundle of exposed nerves. I'd explode all over the place if he didn't stop.

Of course, he didn't. He played my body like Miles Davis played his trumpet. My belly tightened as another orgasm built. I was panting now. Then, his mouth was gone. Before I could breathe a sigh of relief, he pushed two fingers into my dripping pussy alongside the egg.

"Shit!" I yelled when he wiggled his fingers, pushing the egg higher and pressing it against...

A scream exploded from me, echoing around the room. I lost all control. I undulated under the force of the orgasm, and there was nothing I could do to stop my body.

Several minutes later, I floated back to earth. Marcus had removed his fingers and turned the egg off. I couldn't move. Hell, I could barely breathe. Everything tingled. I had never been so aware of my own body. His skin brushed over mine. I forced my eyes open, even though I didn't know when I closed them, to see a satisfied smirk on his face.

"How do you feel?"

"Boneless. Sated."

"Very good." He brushed a kiss over my lax lips. "Have you ever screamed like that before?"

My cheeks grew hot. "No." Of course, I hadn't. I'd never lost control like that. I wasn't sure how I felt about that. In my head, control was everything, but maybe losing it once in a while wasn't a bad thing. Especially since Marcus was able to bring me such pleasure when I let go.

"Another first." He sounded pleased with himself as his fingers traced my damp skin.

My hips shifted, and the egg moved within me. Shivers of pleasure slipped through my veins. "Will you please take that damn egg out." It wasn't a question but a demand.

"Don't you like my toy?"

"Like it yes, but I don't think I can stand another climax without passing out, and if it keeps shifting inside me every time I move, it's going to happen."

"Ah, I see."

He pushed his fingers into my core, and a moan escaped my lips as he slipped the egg out of my dripping sex.

"Thank you."

"You're very welcome." He gave me another light kiss and slid the pillows from beneath my hips, one at a time. Then he covered me with a sheet, even though the room was warm. His tender care almost brought tears to my eyes. I'd never been treated like this before.

"Rest for a few minutes. I'll be right back."

The mattress shifted, but I couldn't move if I wanted to. My muscles were limp, and I was sated. The sound of running water made me want to get up and take a shower, but I didn't think my legs would hold me yet.

The water shut off, and I glanced at the bathroom door. Marcus strode to the bed with a washcloth and towel in his hand. Again. My heart melted. He was so good to me. Always making sure of my comfort. Was this what a relationship was supposed to look like?

He sat on the bed and, with gentle hands, bathed my skin and my sex. I liked being independent, but I also enjoyed the way he took care of me. Marcus took care of me in a way no one ever had, not even my mother.

When he finished, he disappeared into the bathroom again.

I turned my head and found the small clock on the nightstand. Four? It was four in the afternoon? I started to sit up.

"Oh no." He placed his hands on my shoulders. "Continue to rest." He knelt on the mattress and leaned over for a kiss.

I opened my mouth to his, our tongues thrusting against each other, mimicking our earlier lovemaking. I wanted more. More of Marcus and his brand of loving.

He broke the kiss. "Rest." I opened my mouth to say something, but he brushed his lips over mine. "I'm going to start dinner; it will be at least an hour before it's ready. Don't move for at least thirty minutes." He stood and walked toward the door.

My gaze devoured his naked form. "Aren't you going to put some clothes on?"

He winked. "What's the point?" I fell back against the mattress as he left.

I was the most satisfied woman on the planet. Hell, in the whole universe. What did Marcus get out of it? His cock was still hard, and he'd denied his own pleasure to see to me. No man had ever done anything like this before. Even now, he was downstairs cooking and letting me rest.

My pussy clenched thinking about his hard cock thrusting into me. Cripes, how could I want more sex? I'd had what, four, or was it five, orgasms? I should be weary, but my libido was letting me know it was ready to go more rounds with him.

Rolling onto my side, I looked at the clock. Ten minutes had passed. I wanted a shower, not that Marcus hadn't done a good job cleaning me up, but standing under the hot spray would do miracles for my muscles. But could I even stand?

Start off small. I wiggled my toes—they worked. Knees were next—yes, they bent and straightened without problems. I pushed myself onto my elbows and swung my legs over the side of the mattress. Muscles protested, but it wasn't so much pain, rather a pleasant soreness that came from being pleasured over and over again.

I pushed to my feet. I wobbled for a moment before my balance kicked in. Good. Put one foot in front of the other. My legs held as I made my way to the bathroom. Once inside, I gave the big bathtub a loving glance. I didn't have time for the long soak I wanted. Opening the shower door, I stepped inside.

Forty minutes later, I put on a robe, slipped downstairs, my hair still wet, and stood in the doorway of the kitchen, watching Marcus. He stood at the counter with his back to me. My gaze roamed over his nude body. There wasn't an ounce of fat on him, and his firm, hard ass begged for my touch.

His wide shoulders and muscles flexed as he chopped something for dinner. I couldn't stand still, so I padded across the kitchen to him. My fingers traced those muscles, and my lips followed.

"You smell like musk." It wasn't an unpleasant scent—it turned me on.

"I didn't expect you to be down here yet." To his credit, he kept chopping and allowed me to explore him.

"It's a miracle I can do anything after you pleasured me so well." I slipped my arms around his waist, my fingers brushing the head of his hard cock. It twitched beneath my touch. My confidence soared with power.

"Satisfaction is my middle name." His voice was strained.

I knew why. I smiled, loving how my touch affected him. It was a powerful hit of energy.

"Is that so?" Keeping my touch light, I ran the pads of my fingers over his dick. Steel and velvet. His skin was silky, but there was steel underneath as he pulsed against my touch.

God, how long had he been like this? Hours? He deserved to have relief and satisfaction. Oh, yes, I wanted to give him the same pleasure he'd given me. I wanted to see him lose control and climax in my hands. I curled my fingers around his hard dick and stroked him from tip to base and back again.

"Cassie." The knife clattered to the counter.

"Yes, Marcus?" My lips trailed over his well-defined shoulders as I stroked him.

"You're playing with fire."

"It doesn't feel that hot to me." I squeezed his cock and stood on my toes to nibble the back of his neck. "At least, not yet."

Chapter Twenty

♥

C assie

The air in the kitchen thickened, and Marcus stiffened when I tightened my hold on his cock and bit his earlobe, but I had no plans to stop. I enjoyed the power flowing through me at having him in my hand, his libido under my control. My nipples tightened, and my pussy moistened while I stroked him, his hardness pulsing with need.

I've accepted that this weekend was the best thing I'd ever been convinced to try. There was still a part of me that was apprehensive, though. I needed to let myself go, to have sex without remorse or fear. To trust Marcus and enjoy myself for once.

His hand closed over mine, then gently pulled it from his twitching cock. He turned to face me.

"I want to touch you." I wanted his skin against mine, his cock in my hand.

"I don't know if I can handle any more touching right now." He brought my hand up to his lips, placing a soul-destroying kiss in the center of my palm.

"Sure, you can." With my free hand, I found his dick. His groan was lost against the palm of my hand as he held it against his mouth. A grin crossed my lips. "Why don't we try this?" I tugged my hand free. Before he could react, I kneeled and took his dick deep into my mouth.

I wanted to suck him off. I wanted him to climax and get some satisfaction. This was only my second time going down on a man. Correction, second time doing it to him, to any man. Last time, he'd pulled me off before he finished. His salty taste wasn't unpleasant, and I inhaled. His musky scent—along with a hint of spice—filled me. Yes, this man was spicy all right. I ran my tongue over the veins of his cock.

His fingers tangled in my hair, and a sense of control made me bolder. He wasn't trying to pull me away, but keeping me close.

"Oh yes, baby. Suck me." He thrust deeper.

I relaxed my throat and took him in. An image popped into my mind from an article I'd read at work. I pressed my finger to his perineum and waited in anticipation.

"Fuck!" he cried out. I didn't have to wait long. His balls tightened, and his salty fluid filled my mouth.

I swallowed, loving every second of the empowerment I'd never felt before rush through my veins. I'd made him lose control. Maybe not for long, but I'd done it.

Me.

His cock finished pulsing, and I encircled the head before I let him slip from my mouth.

His hand tightened in my hair as he urged me to my feet, then covered my mouth with his. I started to pull back, but his hands against my head held me fast. Apparently, he didn't mind his taste on my tongue as he thrust deep into my mouth. When he broke the kiss, we were both breathing heavily.

"Why did you bother to put a robe on?" He fingered the collar of the light pink material.

"I can't run around naked."

"You should try it." His fingers parted the lapels and cupped my breasts, the slight roughness of his palms against my soft skin sending shivers of delight through me. "It's very freeing."

He pinched my nipples, and my moan was lost against his lips when he kissed me again. Our hips rocked against each other as our tongues tangled.

His green eyes were blazing when he lifted his head to stare down at me. "If we don't stop, I'm going to take you on the kitchen counter."

"Is that a problem?" Where had this vixen come from? I had no idea, but I was beginning to like the new me. His eyes darkened, and fire spread through me when I realized I'd made him lose control. Power rushed to my head. Wiggling, I pushed my hand between us and cupped his growing sex.

"You're asking for trouble."

"I like trouble."

Before I could blink, I was flat on my back on the island in the middle of the kitchen, my legs hanging over the edge, robe spread apart, and Marcus between my thighs.

His cock rubbed at my entrance, then he thrust. My back arched as my pussy opened to him. Oh, God. My mouth dropped open. He was so large, so hard, so male. There were no other words I could think of to describe the delicious sensations coursing through me.

Marcus gripped my hips. "Get ready for a hard ride."

I closed my eyes as he pistoned in and out of my pussy. I curled my legs around his waist, and crossed my ankles at the small of his back.

He felt so fucking good. "Please, take me."

Chapter Twenty-One

♥

Marcus

The little witch shattered my control. I thrust into her warm and willing pussy. She'd done something no other woman had ever managed to do: make me come against my choice and in a short period of time, too. Even now, I was completely buried in her silky, warm cunt, and I couldn't stop from thrusting harder and faster. When she wrapped her legs around my waist, I leaned forward and captured her lips.

My tongue mimicked my cock, thrusting into her mouth, tasting every part of her. Her pussy clenched around me. Cassie didn't have a clue what she'd done. Maybe that wasn't a bad thing. I was having trouble keeping my dominant side controlled because of her actions. I wasn't one to let someone else take the reins, but damn if she wasn't sexy doing it.

The dominant side wanted my due, and I wasn't going to stop until I got it. Her first climax made me lick my lips; her second caused me to grin. It wasn't until her pussy constricted for a third time that my body agreed it was time.

I reached between our bodies, found her clit, and pressed it as I thrust into her. She screamed out my name, throwing her head back. I roared as my release flowed out of me. I pulsed again and again inside her pussy.

It could have been a minute or an hour before we both stopped shaking from the force of our respective climaxes.

I lifted my head. Her eyes were closed, her mouth open, and her breathing shallow. My chest rose and fell in rapid response. "Are you okay?" My voice was hoarse.

"Peachy." Her pale blue eyes met my gaze. Her lips were puffy from my hard kisses, but a tiny smile played around her lips.

"Did I hurt you?" I hadn't been gentle. I went to pull out of her only to realize her legs were still wrapped around my waist.

"Nope. You didn't hurt me, and I think I finally uncovered the volcano."

She flexed her hips, and damn if my dick didn't respond.

Control. We both needed time to recover, but from the way my cock was twitching, it didn't want or need anything except her.

While I was trying to figure out a way to disengage myself, her stomach rumbled.

I chuckled and placed a soft kiss on her belly. "Baby, you need to release me so I can finish fixing us dinner. I think someone is hungry."

"You feel too good." Her hips flexed again, and her legs tightened.

"Food first, then we can have some more fun."

She pouted at me, but her legs slipped from my waist. I caught them with my arms and lowered them with care as I stepped back. I reached for her hands and helped her sit up. I'd never look at that island again without thinking of her spread out on it, ready for my pleasure.

"Baby," I said when her fingers slipped from mine to my half-erect dick. I reached down and removed her hand. "Keep your hands to yourself." No matter how good it felt, I had to get her to stop touching me or we'd never eat.

"Spoilsport." She slid off the counter to her feet, and I gripped her around the waist when she wobbled. I pulled her robe off the island and rested it on her shoulders. She shrugged into it. I tied it shut. Not because I wanted to, but it was better if her lush curves were covered for now.

Her stomach growled again. "I guess you better feed us or we'll never get to the fun."

"Food coming right up." I forced myself to push away from her. I washed my hands and went back to the cutting board to finish up our meal.

"Do you have disinfectant wipes?"

I glanced over my shoulder at her. "In the left cabinet under the island."

She squatted, pulled the wipes out, then proceeded to sanitize the island. I turned back to focus on what I was chopping before I sliced my finger open. I finished with the vegetables and heard the cabinet bang shut.

"Can I help you with anything?"

"No." I stayed facing the counter because my damn cock wouldn't go down. "Actually, you can set the table. In the dining room, you'll find the cabinet with everything in it. The drawers have utensils, place mats, and all that stuff."

"Off I go."

I let out a breath as she bounced out of the kitchen. Maybe now I could convince my dick to settle down and finish dinner. Maybe being nude wasn't such a good idea.

Chapter Twenty-Two

♥

Marcus

I watched as Cassie ate dinner with relish. Thankfully, our impromptu kitchen sex hadn't ruined dinner. I kept my gaze on her and thought out about dessert. Maybe I'd spread her on the table, scoop ice cream onto her breasts, stomach, and pussy, then lick it off as it melted.

My cock jumped. Not yet. I relaxed back in my chair and cradled my wine glass in my hand.

"Another great meal." Cassie set her fork down and wiped her lips with a napkin.

I inclined my head and stared at her. Right now, she showed me yet a different side of herself. Cassie was relaxed and open, compared to the sexy wildcat earlier and compared to yesterday's uptight, closed woman. She had a way of putting on different faces, some of them filled with fear and anxiety.

I would get to the bottom of that.

"Today is the first time you've let your control slip," I commented. We had control issues in common, but why did she feel the need to maintain such restraint?

The smile on her face faded. Damn, maybe I shouldn't have asked, but we needed to get this out in the open. She pushed her chair back, and... Maybe I'd lost any ground I'd made by bringing this up.

I blew out a breath. "Cassie?"

She stood, but before she could take a step, I was in front of her. I grabbed her arms, and she pulled away.

"I don't want to talk about it."

Her voice was strong. That was a good thing. I wasn't going to let her hide, not yet.

"What has you so afraid of losing control?"

"I could ask you the same thing!" She crossed her arms over her chest and gave me a mutinous stare. She hadn't answered my question but posed one of her own. With a gentle touch, I guided her into the family room and to the sofa.

I put my arm along the back as we sat. Close, but not too close. I wanted her smile back, and maybe I could do that with my honesty. "I've lost control with you. We're all afraid of something." I tilted my head.

"Right." The word was hard, but her shoulders sagged just a bit.

"Some may not admit it. I will. For me, it's spiders. I hate the things. I have this place debugged, so to speak, every month." I ran my fingers over her neck.

She shivered before a giggle escaped her lips, and her shoulders shifted before she relaxed.

Good. I didn't want her feeling defensive, but I wanted to find out what was going on inside that mind of hers. There was something in the way she watched me that told me she wasn't going to answer my questions.

This conversation would go nowhere right now. Not until I could get her to let her guard down...

A thought popped into my brain.

"I'm going to clean up the dishes. Why don't you go into the library?" She always had her nose in a book when she ate lunch in the break room. Maybe that would help her relax.

"Library?" Her eyes narrowed. "You have a library and didn't tell me?"

"I forgot, and I didn't think we'd have a lot of time for reading."

I took her hand, led her down the hall, and opened the door to the library. I was proud of this room. Floor-to-ceiling bookcases, all full of books, everything from fiction to non-fiction, including history tomes, biographies, and lots of books about sex. Reading helped me relax.

Maybe it would help her do the same. "Have fun."

I left her standing inside the room with her mouth agape.

Whistling, I strode down the hall to the dining room.

Chapter Twenty-Three

❤

C assie

I wandered around Marcus' library. The wooden shelves were overflowing with books laying sideways on top of books, as well as a few piles on low tables that edged the shelves. Compared to his bedroom not as tidy. Marcus was a complicated man, as if I didn't already know that.

I had no clue about his cooking abilities until this weekend, and now his library. It was all so confusing, but a part of learning about him. I took in the sitting area in the middle of the room held a sofa and two over-stuffed chairs. There were two side tables with lamps on them, perfect for curling up with a good book. A very impressive library.

My fingers trailed along the spines as I looked at the titles. There were great literary works, mysteries, thrillers, history, and even some romances.

But what drew my attention the most was the bookcases filled with erotic books.

Erotic romances, how-to-books, erotica, and even what looked like some porn. One of the titles caught my eye: *The Submissive Has All The Control.*

My heart pounded as I plucked it off the shelf.

Marcus wanted a submissive. That was pretty easy to tell. I'd had no time to think anything through, but one thing I knew for certain—I cared about Marcus.

Maybe even more than cared.

Could I cede power to him? Submit?

I shook my head. Memories and fears reared up inside me.

I started to put the book back, then froze. If I couldn't sort this out, there was no chance for Marcus and me, and I wanted that chance. I really did.

Taking a deep breath, I took the book to the sofa, curled up, opened it with trembling hands, and started to read.

"Hey."

My head snapped up. How long had I been reading? My cheeks warmed seeing Marcus lounging in the doorway.

Had he noticed what I was reading? I tucked the book face down next to my leg.

His eyes gleamed. "I didn't mean to disturb you. I only wanted to let you know I'm going upstairs to get the bedroom ready."

"Ready for what?" My stomach clenched, and I forced myself to take a deep breath and let it out. He'd only shown me pleasure so far.

But had he seen the title of the book I was reading?

I studied his face. It revealed nothing. Maybe he hadn't been there long enough to read the title.

"My surprise," he said. "Don't come up until I call for you." He sauntered off, and I stared at the empty doorway for a minute or two before I picked the book back up.

After reading the first few chapters, I could see differences between Marcus and my father. I still didn't understand my mother's acceptance, and I wasn't sure I wanted to.

Marcus was a Dominant—there was no doubt in my mind about it. But in a totally different way than my father. Marcus didn't hit me or verbally abuse me in any way. That difference made me feel better. When I'd taken control in the kitchen, he'd taken it right back, and the world hadn't fallen apart. In fact, I'd enjoyed that little soiree. A lot.

A tingle of excitement crawled through my veins. I couldn't ask for a better lover than Marcus. Not only did he make sure I was well satisfied, he took care of me like no other man ever had. There was something tender in the way he touched me, in his gaze, in his kisses. Oh, he could be a little rough with sex, but I didn't mind.

And the pleasure. He enjoyed making me climax even while denying himself. One of the lines from the book stood out in my mind.

An excellent Dom will make sure his submissive is happy.

Marcus made me happy. I wasn't convinced yet that I was any sort of submissive, but the book pointed out there were different types of submission. Who knew? There was the slave who was totally submissive to their Master—twenty-four/seven—and had almost no voice. That had been my mother.

Then there was the sexual submissive who submitted only in the bedroom, plus those who only showed submission in the home and not in public.

I was sure there were more, but those three made sense to me. The book also talked about the power exchange between sub and Dom. How trust in your partner was not only powerful, it would make the relationship stronger, closer, and sexier.

My stomach contracted. While my mind might deny it, my gut knew Marcus was an alpha male, one who would not only take care of me physically, but mentally as well. He was a man I could put my trust in, and I knew that.

So why did my heart pound so hard when I considered submitting?

Could I do this? Trust a dominant man?

Marcus' voice rang down the stairs and into the library. "Cassie, you can come upstairs now."

There was no time left to think this through. I needed to make a decision.

Heart beating triple time and my lungs struggling to get enough air, I climbed the stairs to the bedroom. What little air I had rushed out of my lungs as I stepped inside the bedroom. The room was bathed in candlelight, and Marcus stood next to the bed, gloriously naked.

With determination, I walked across the room, discarded my robe and stood in front of him. I was distracted by the towel-covered nightstand. What did he have hidden there? Anticipation with a tinge of fear worked its way up my spine.

He scooped me into his arms, and the next thing I knew I was lying in the middle of the bed with Marcus straddling me. My heart pounded hard. I opened my mouth.

"*Shhh.*" He brushed a light kiss against my lips.

I shook my head moving away from his kisses. "I need to say this." I took a deep breath. I needed to trust him and that meant taking this first step. "You're the first man I've never had to fake an orgasm with."

There, it was out.

His features went stone cold. "Those others were fucking idiots."

I couldn't help but smile at his words.

"The men in your past didn't know what a treasure they had in you."

"Maybe." My teeth dug into my lower lip. "It might have been that I was too afraid to let them give me one."

Marcus' head jerked up, and he stiffened. Well I had his attention now. I wasn't sure if that was a good thing or not, but he wanted to know, and I was ready to give him some information.

He shifted off my body and slid to my side, cradling me against him. He reached for the sheet, but I pushed his hand away.

"You were right when you said I was afraid of losing control." Lord, it was hard to admit this out loud. "Until now, I saw losing control as being associated with pain."

"I would never hurt you."

"I know that. I think. At least, I'm trying to. But I can't just let go of a feeling I've lived with so long. I've tried."

"Is that why you were talking to Josh?"

It didn't surprise me he'd figured out that I'd wanted to try anonymous sex. Marcus was a smart man. He'd put two and two together. I nodded. There was no reason to deny it. A weight inside me slid away.

"How did you find out about that?" I'd hoped he didn't know about that. It was out of character for me to go to Josh, but I'd needed to get Marcus out of my head.

Marcus blew out a breath. "I saw you two talking, and it was an educated guess."

I believed him. I might as well get this out of the way. "Until this weekend, I thought maybe having anonymous sex would be the ticket to helping me get past my fears. Within five minutes of our deal, I knew I wouldn't go through with it, and I called Josh and told him to ignore my request."

Marcus' green eyes softened. "What has helped you understand your need for control?"

"For a long time, I shut it out and didn't try to understand it. Lately, I've been thinking about it a lot."

A quick smile broke the seriousness on his face. "Because of me?"

I wasn't quite ready to have that discussion. Hell, I hadn't even figured that out for myself.

"Maybe. Today, though, reading a book from your library opened my eyes and helped me understand certain things I didn't before."

"Which book?"

"It doesn't matter." So, he hadn't seen the title. Good. I wasn't quite ready to share it with him. "While I can't say I won't be afraid of losing my control, I know I'm safe with you if I do."

"You'll always be safe with me." He gave me another soft kiss. "That's the reason I use a safe word. Any decent Dom would. It gives you the control to stop whatever is happening, no matter what."

I nodded as tears crowded my throat. From all my interactions with my father, and the things I'd heard him do to my mother—and seeing the results—if my mother had a safe word, or one my father had respected, maybe things wouldn't have been so bad.

But from everything I read, my mother was more like a slave, with no voice at all, to my abusive father. There was no way I would ever be like that.

"How do you feel about being restrained?"

I closed my eyes and reopened them, processing his words.

"Your skin is flushing. Shall I take that as a yes?"

"I've never tried it." My nerves tingled.

"Have you fantasized about it?"

"Yes." I had, and he'd been starring in those fantasies. Now he was going to make them come true.

"Let's see how this goes. Put your arms above your head."

Nerves pulsing. I raised my arms. Marcus leaned over me, his chest brushing against my breasts. Softness surrounded my wrists and then a distinct metal click sounded. I tugged—a natural reaction. But instead of the cold steel I expected to cut into my wrists, a velvet softness pressed against my skin.

A comforting softness.

I tugged again. I couldn't get loose and took a shaky breath.

"I've run the handcuff links between the slats on the headboard." His voice was husky. "The cuffs themselves are fur-lined, so they won't mark your beautiful skin. Are you all right?"

"So far."

His lips and tongue followed a path from the cuff on my right wrist all the way to my shoulder, leaving a path of blazing arousal.

I turned my head and our gazes clashed. "Are you going to let me see what's on the nightstand?" I jerked my chin in that direction.

"No." He took my lips, tongue diving into my mouth, tangling with mine before withdrawing. "Lift your head, please."

I dropped my chin to my chest and fabric covered my eyes.

"No." I jerked against the handcuffs, my breathing shallow and sweat breaking out on my skin. "Michelle, Michelle, Michelle!"

I couldn't control my body movements. I tugged at the handcuffs and thrashed around on the bed. My heart racing.

The blindfold was taken away, and Marcus stared at me with concern etched on his face. His fingers brushed my hair away from my forehead before he stroked my cheek. "Sweetheart?"

I fought to get my breathing and panic under control. "My father used to blindfold me to punish me and then tie my hands behind my back to stop me from removing it. It's the reason I can't stand total darkness."

Marcus swore. "I'm sorry, baby. I had no idea he hurt you that way." His breath was cool against my heated skin and his touch gentle.

I appreciated his tender touch as it was helping me to calm down. Marcus listened to me and reacted to my safe word. That alone helped my heart rate settle a bit.

"Do you want me to remove the cuffs as well?"

I took a deep breath. "They're okay. No blindfold." The loss of my sight had made me panic, not the restraints.

"Not a problem." He tossed the fabric away. "Can you keep your eyes closed?"

"Why?"

"Because I don't want you to see what is coming. I want you to use your other senses rather than sight. Trust me. I won't hurt you."

"I'll do my best." I let my lashes fall. I could handle that. Besides, I could open my eyes at any time, and the room was lit.

Chapter Twenty-Four

♥

Marcus

My fingers clenched at my sides while I fought to keep my anger at bay over how Cassie's father treated her. How dare any man blindfold and restrain a child as a punishment! Taking a deep breath, I maneuvered until I faced her feet.

I kissed her toes, and she wiggled her feet. Reaching over, I pulled out the leg restraints and secured one ankle. "Okay?" I turned my head, and she nodded. I secured her other ankle.

I glanced over my shoulder again, and I was pleased to see her eyes were still closed. Her nose was wrinkled as if she was thinking about what I was doing. When I tightened the leg restraints, a small tremor shook her, but she didn't say a word.

"Are you okay?" I asked when I had the restraints as tight as I wanted them.

"Fine." Her voice was breathless.

I moved so I could watch her face. I trailed my fingers from her ankle to her knee, watching her face. No fear, no apprehension, and her skin was flushed from excitement.

"You said you fantasized about being tied up?"

"Yes."

"You'll have to tell me some of your other fantasies so I can fulfill them for you."

A tremor swept over her body. She reacted to my words. Good. My cock was hard again. Hell, who was I kidding? I'd been in a constant state of arousal since the company party months ago. I was a highly sexual male, but I'd never been this hard, this often around a woman.

Only Cassie.

Slipping off the bed, I took the towel off the nightstand and lifted the feather I wanted, then ran it over her lips.

Her mouth puckered against it before I trailed it over her neck, to her breasts, carefully caressing each one before I teased her nipples.

"What is that?" She squirmed against the sheets.

"You tell me." Leaving her breasts, I trailed the feather over her stomach, past her sex to her thighs, then to her knees and feet, before reversing course. Goosebumps skittered across her skin, and her hips were shifting as I made my way up her body. I smelled the sweet, musky perfume of her arousal.

That's what I wanted—I wanted her aroused.

"Is it a feather?"

"Yes." Dropping a kiss on her abdomen, I put the feather back and picked up a pair of vibrating eggs. "Let's see if you can tell what this is." I took one of the eggs and rubbed it against her clit.

Her hips shifted. "A dildo?"

"No." I pressed it into her wetness, then drew it out, only to slide it back in, watching her face. She was being so good. Her eyes were still closed and pride swelled in me.

"Too small for a dildo." Her forehead wrinkled. "It's something small and round. Maybe something for a woman who doesn't want something too big? Yet she wants something to make her feel good."

I was impressed. She was reasoning this out. "You are close. Do you remember what we give our clients when they first come to Fantasies, Inc.?"

"Oh my God, you have one of those toys the women rave about. Smaller than what you used in the shower yesterday, but I've heard it's more powerful. I've never seen one."

"Yes, it's one of those special toys. I'm surprised you've never seen it." Why did that surprise me?

"I haven't looked at it. But the women call with compliments all the time." Her breath grew choppy as I shifted the toy. "You're a wicked man."

"You haven't seen anything yet."

We were going to have *so* much fun.

Chapter Twenty-Five

♥

C assie

I lay on the mattress, fighting to keep my eyes closed as my heart rate increased at Marcus' words.

You haven't seen anything yet.

My blood heated in my veins as I gave myself over to him, mentally, emotionally, and physically. "Go for it," I said.

"I plan to."

His words sent shivers of desire throughout my body. I heard him rustling around, the mattress dipping with his movements, and I was tempted to take a peek, but I didn't. I'd given my word to keep my eyes closed the best I could, and I would.

Another feather whisked over my already hard nipples, to my belly, making my skin prickle with excitement.

Wait a second. This had a different feel to it. Round feathers? Maybe it was a ball covered with feathers. I couldn't figure it out. He rubbed my stomach with it and then pressed against my pussy lips.

A small vibrator? It had that shape and feel to it. But then the vibrator and the feather ball shifted at the same time. The more the vibrator was pushed into my pussy, the closer the feather ball shifted to my clit.

My hips jerked when he flipped the vibrator on, and the feather ball moved on my clit. The feathers teased me in a soft manner, and the vibrator caused my pussy to clench around it. I was caught between laughing and moaning. What a diabolical toy.

"You're shameless," I said, fighting to keep my body still.

Marcus chuckled and pulled the vibrator out only to thrust it back in to my wet pussy. The feather ball teased my clit even more. "Do you like my toy? This is one of my newest inventions. The feathers are synthetic so they don't wet and sticky. How long can you hold out?"

His teasing tone had me biting my lip, so I didn't answer him. My body was already primed and ready, and he knew it. I wasn't going to last long. I wasn't sure if that was good or bad. All I knew was that payback was going to be fun.

The mounting pleasure was so delicious. He kept teasing me with the vibrator and the ball. I jerked at my hands, wanting to touch him, to feel his skin beneath my fingers, but I couldn't. I started to close my legs, then remembered I was restrained there as well. Frustration rose through me. I wanted to rock my hips so I could come faster.

I was restrained by an expert. Marcus could do anything he wanted to me, and I couldn't stop him. A tremor of fear shuddered up my spine until I remembered I had my safe word. He'd already proven he would stop when I said it. There was nothing to fear.

A shaft of pleasure shot from pussy to nipples. "Release my hand." I didn't care about the demanding tone of my voice.

"No."

"You're not playing fair. I want to touch you." I flexed my fingers.

"I never said I play fair, and I like having you at my mercy." There was a hint of laughter in his voice.

"Damn it, Marcus." I tugged at the handcuffs.

"Such language."

"Just wait. I'll pay you back for this." I would. I'd find a way this weekend to get even with him.

The mattress dipped. "I look forward to you getting even." His breath brushed my ear. "Anytime you want me to stop, say your safe word."

The *pop* of a lid almost made me open my eyes. He pulled the vibrator out of my pussy and the ball left my clit.

Damn, I was so close. I almost demanded he put it back. Something wet dribbled down my mound to my pussy. As if I wasn't wet enough. Marcus rubbed the moisture on my clit and over my labia. He slipped two fingers into my pussy and twirled them around.

I couldn't stop my hips from shifting upward, not that I could get a lot of air between me and the mattress. No, he'd restrained me too well. A scent of roses filled my nose when I inhaled.

"Rose oil?" It was a guess since I kept my eyes closed.

"A very special rose oil."

Now, what did *that* mean? My stomach tightened as warmth began to spread through my pussy, to my clit, and throughout my body.

"What is it?" I wiggled my ass against the sheets. The rose oil was getting hotter by the minute. It wasn't an unpleasant feeling, and it made my nerves dance with anticipation.

"Warming oil. A little something to keep you on edge."

His fingers were spreading my labia open, and he pressed a new toy against my pussy. I tried to concentrate on the shape and feel of the new toy, but the warmth spreading through my limbs was distracting.

"Another one of your inventions?" My breathing grew shallow in anticipation of what he had planned for me.

"One of my engineers came up with this one."

There was pride in his voice. There was a slight pinch to my clit, and I let out a moan. His fingers against my abdomen made me shiver, then the toy shifted, and the pinch was replaced with a strong tug on my clit.

I sucked in a breath, trying to process what was happening. The toy was switched on. "*Ahhh!*" I cried out. It was like there was a mouth on my clit, sucking then releasing. The warming oil increased the sensations and sensitivity to my clit.

"I'll have to let my engineer know about the adjustments I just made."

"What the hell is that thing?" I could barely get the words out. God, he was going to kill me with pleasure. Blood pumped though my veins straight from pussy to clit.

"It's a fun little toy." The pressure on my clit increased, and my ass wiggled as if I could dislodge it. "In our focus groups," Marcus continued, "women complained that toys didn't have enough suction to re-create the feeling of a lover sucking their clit. One of my engineers began to make some modifications."

"Oh hell, this thing is..." My back arched as much as it could, then settled back against the mattress as my body reacted. "Diabolical," I panted.

I was so close; I was going to climax any second now, and there was nothing I could do to hold it back. My body was on fire.

"Interesting word choice." He slid between my spread legs.

"Oh yes," I whispered when his cock touched my entrance. "Yes, please, fuck me." I wanted his hard cock in me when I went over the edge.

Chapter Twenty-Six

♥

Marcus

Cassie was wet and yet so snug as I pushed my cock into her pussy. I would need to be careful not to dislodge the toy. Moving with care, I slid fully into her pussy and turned the clit sucker up another notch.

Cassie bucked against me. I pulled back, then began stroking in and out in a measured pace. Every few strokes, I'd increase the sucker on her clit, and my cock would jump at her little cries of pleasure and need. The warming oil on her clit was doing its job. My heart picked up speed when she undulated beneath me as much as the restraints would allow you.

Damn, she looked good tied up in my bed. I wanted to keep her there. I wanted more than just a weekend with her; I wanted a lifetime.

"Please," she whispered as her pussy tightened around my dick.

"Please, what?" I wanted her to learn to voice her need, her wants with me.

"Fuck me. Make me come before I go crazy."

A moan escaped her lips when I slid deep, filling her. I leaned down and captured the next moan with my mouth. I kissed her softly before I trailed my lips from hers over her cheek to her ear. "Your wish is my command," I whispered in her ear.

I pulled back and thrust deeply into her wet depths and kept an eye on the toy to make sure it stayed in place. It shouldn't fall off, not with the suction, but I still wanted to make sure I didn't hurt Cassie. She was too precious to hurt.

"Harder," she cried out, her arms and legs jerking in the cuffs.

A grin crept over my lips at her command, but I didn't increase my pace. I was in control, and she was going to learn that.

"Oh, God. Please. I need you."

There it was.

Her surrender.

I heard it in her voice. I pounded into her while I turned the suction on the toy to the next level.

"Almost there," she whispered as our hips met.

"You're so fucking beautiful." I brushed another kiss over her lips, then her scrunched-shut eyes. My beauty was fighting her release. Her pussy clenched around me and then released, only to spasm harder. I fought against my own release, surprising for me. "Let it go, baby, come for me. Show me the beauty of your climax. Let me see you go wild." I pushed the toy to its maximum.

Cassie jerked as I slammed into her. Her body stiffened, and she screamed as her orgasm hit. I continued to thrust until a second climax took over, then I sank into her and let my own take over. It was at the last second that I remembered to switch the sucker off.

When I finished pulsing into her, I laid over her body and our harsh breathing filled the room. Her pussy twitched. I wanted to stay buried in her for the rest of day but... I started to pull back.

"No." The cuffs rattled against the headboard. "Stay, at least for a few more minutes."

My heart melted at her words. Reaching up, I brushed her hair away from her face. "You can open your eyes now."

A giggle escaped her as a drowsy blue gaze met mine. "I'd forgotten I'd closed them."

"Okay?" I'd been a little rough with her.

"Perfect." Her pussy tightened again.

"Keep that up and I'm going to fuck you again." I couldn't seem to get enough of her. Cassie was the first woman who'd made me lose control. I filed that thought away for later.

"I wouldn't mind, but this time I want to be able to touch you and wrap my legs around you." She kissed my chin. "I also want to keep my eyes open so I can see you fly apart."

"Deal." I pulled from her willing body and released the restraints. "Take a deep breath."

She did, and I released the sucker. I gently lifted it from her clit, which was red and inflamed. "I think we could both use some recovery time." I tossed the toy on the nightstand. I wasn't sure I needed to recover, but I didn't want to rush her. Her clit was going to be very sensitive.

"I'm sure we can pass the time."

"Yes, we can." My lips captured hers, a swell of emotion almost overwhelming me. Empowerment I'd never felt rushed through me. Cassie had trusted me and wanted more. The woman of my dreams was mine. Nothing would change my mind.

We were both breathing hard when I broke the kiss.

"Tell me more about yourself," she said.

"What do you want to know?" I rolled onto my back, pulling her with me until she laid with her head on my shoulder, her arm over my chest.

"Parents?"

"Two." Her soft laughter warmed my heart. "My parents are both still alive. Right now, they're on a European cruise, enjoying their retirement."

"How do they handle you working for Fantasies, Inc.?"

"They're both happy I've found a creative outlet for my experiments."

"They know about your sex toys?" Her eyes were bright and curious, and I realized she was comparing my upbringing to hers.

"Yes, they are aware of what I do. I think they're glad I stopped blowing stuff up and found a place that makes me happy."

"Why do I have a feeling you played with chemistry sets as a child?" She snuggled closer to my body, and her breasts pressed against my skin. The sensation of her fingers tracing circles on my chest felt amazing.

"Chemistry sets, experiments on the stove. I'd tie my friends up to see if the knots would hold. Oh, and I accidentally set the dog house on fire."

"How do you *accidentally* do that?" She tilted her head up, her eyes twinkling with interest.

"I was playing with candles and wax. How the heck did I know at the ripe old age of ten that wax could burn that hot when it hit the skin? I knocked over the candle, which caught the dog bed on fire, then the dog house."

"And the dog?"

"He was outside whining because I'd kicked him out to play." I grinned at the memory. It had been a long time since I'd thought about my childhood.

"What did your parents do?"

"Called the fire department, and after they left, I was given a lecture about playing with matches and candles. They grounded me for two weeks, and I had to pay for the wood and build the new dog house."

"Your parents sound wonderful."

"They were fair and understanding." Was I doing the right thing, explaining about my normal childhood? Something I had a feeling she hadn't had with her parents. In time, I'd get to hear her full story, when she was ready to talk to me about it. I searched her face for sadness and found none. Maybe she'd begun to let that go?

"You really enjoy your job at Fantasies, Inc. don't you?" Her voice sounded sleepy as she snuggled closer.

My dick reacted, and I pushed down my need. This was about Cassie.

"Yes, I love creating toys for both men and women, but you want to know the best thing about the job?" I'd never been one for pillow talk, but with Cassie, it was different. Relaxing. And it brought us closer together.

"Sure."

"It was meeting you and being able to see you every day."

I waited for her reaction, but she was silent. I glanced down and smiled. She'd fallen asleep. I tightened my arms around her. I'd lay here with her and plan out our day tomorrow, because I intended to keep her busy, in and out of bed.

Chapter Twenty-Seven

♥

Cassie

I woke in Marcus' arms. The candles had been blown out, but he'd left the bathroom light on, which warmed my heart. He was so good to and for me. I shifted and looked at the clock. Five. Way too early in the morning to be awake, but I knew I wouldn't go back to sleep.

Once I woke, I rarely went back to sleep. Not wanting to disturb Marcus, I carefully slipped from his embrace and off the bed. I found my robe, wrapped it around my body, and walked over to the window seat.

I was in trouble. *Deep* trouble. Hell, who was I kidding? I'd been in trouble for a while now.

I was falling in love with Marcus.

I gazed out at the sky filled with stars in the early spring morning.

I'd agreed to this weekend to get him out of my system. Instead, he was becoming more ingrained in my life. More essential to my happiness. There was something freeing in telling him about my father blindfolding me as a punishment. It still surprised me that I'd told him. And my trust in him when he tied me up...

I never expected it to be so exciting, so erotic.

After we had mind-blowing sex last night, he held me in his arms and we talked. Actually talked about his life. That was a first for me, and our connection grew so much stronger because of it. It scared me how much I was beginning to care.

It scared me a lot.

When he said I was the reason he loved work, it spooked me. I wasn't ready for this, but I also didn't want to hurt his feelings. I needed time. So I faked being asleep.

This man was everything I could ask for: witty, intelligent, sexy, and an imaginative lover.

Boy, was *that* an understatement.

How was I going to leave him Monday morning? I didn't have a choice. We could never have a life together. I wouldn't live with a dominant man, not without fear of losing myself in the process.

He would eventually get tired of the tug of war between us when I couldn't submit to him all the time. Plus, he was getting emotionally involved. He didn't need a woman like me in his life. After I'd read the book in his library, it had become very apparent that my father used sex and his toys like weapons, not to enhance pleasure, and my mother let my father control her. Or was unable—or unwilling—to escape his control."

I refused to let that happen to me.

Glancing at the bed, I smiled at seeing Marcus spread out over the sheets, his dark hair tousled, and for once, his cock didn't tent the fabric. I'd savor this time with him. We'd agreed to the sixty hours, and I wasn't going to trade this time for anything.

Funny how I'd almost forgotten about that crazy deal. My heart might break into pieces after tomorrow, but I'd deal with it, just like I'd dealt with all the other heartbreak in my life.

For now, we still had time.

Decision made, I wanted to relish our time together.

A grin formed along with an idea. I crossed the room back to the bed and lowered the sheet, exposing his nude body. My mouth watered. *Payback is a bitch.* I found the restraints for his legs. With care, I slipped the first one over his ankle. When he didn't move, I moved to his other ankle. I was careful not to fasten them too tightly, and keep the key to unlock them within reach.

Passion slipped through me as I spied the handcuffs, still threaded through the headboard. I winced when I lifted them, and the metal rattled against the wood. There was some slack for me to lift them but not much.

Marcus had thrown one arm over his head. That would be the easy one, but what about the other? It lay over his washboard stomach. If I lifted it, he'd wake up.

Hmm. I snapped the cuff quietly on one wrist, then leaned down.

"Marcus," I whispered in his ear. "Sweetheart, I need you to move your arm."

He shifted in his sleep, and his arm fell from his stomach to his side. Not what I was hoping for, but I could work with it. I trailed my fingers from his shoulder to his hand, keeping my gaze on his face. I shifted his arm up and over his head.

"Cassie," he murmured, shifting.

"I'm here." I brushed a kiss against his dream-softened lips. "Just getting comfortable."

"*Hmm*." His arm relaxed, allowing me to maneuver it into place. I locked his second wrist into the cuff. *Yes*. I almost pumped my fists in victory, but I wasn't done yet. I shifted to the end of the bed and slowly tightened the leg restraints. I didn't tighten them all the way, but enough he shouldn't be able to get loose.

Marcus was going to have a surprise when he woke.

Taking my robe off, I tossed it on the chair, then climbed back onto the mattress, between his legs. I laid my head on his hip and circled the base of his cock with my hand. Oh, this was going to be fun. I lowered my mouth.

Let's see how he likes this wake-up call.

Chapter Twenty-Eight

♥

Marcus

Something soft and wet covered my cock, which roared to attention. Damn, but it felt good.

I tugged at my hand. It wouldn't move.

I forced my eyes open. The sight of Cassie's head over my cock surprised me, but it shouldn't have. We'd spent another night together, and she was getting more adventurous when it came to sex. I attempted to move my hands so I could tangle my fingers in her hair.

And they didn't budge.

What the hell? I tilted my head and saw the cuffs around my wrists.

She'd *cuffed* me?

Somehow, while I was sleeping, she managed to get the cuffs around my wrists without me knowing about it.

How had she managed it? Maybe because, for the first time in my life, I was totally relaxed around a woman who wasn't my mother. Cassie had wormed her way into my heart and soul.

I shifted my legs. Damn, she was good. I was a light sleeper, yet she'd restrained my legs as well. Score one for her.

Her tongue swirled around the head of my cock, and I hardened more. I fought against a natural urge to struggle against the bonds. I'd never let anyone restrain me before.

As a Dominant, I could permit anything I wanted, and I sensed Cassie needed this. So I'd allow it. She needed at least one time to have me in her control.

I forced myself to relax and let her pleasure me. To show her that I trusted her. Completely.

The thought didn't shock me as it once might have. Trust wasn't something I gave to a woman, especially since the last woman in my life betrayed me by trying to destroy my special room. But I trusted Cassie.

Who was I kidding?

I was in love with her. Otherwise, I never would have mentioned my family. Or slept so soundly she could restrain me.

My sixty-hour challenge had only been a means to the end, a way of getting her into my territory. I'd convince her tomorrow that this didn't have to be the end, but a beginning. She needed me as much as I needed her, so I wasn't going to give up.

Her fingers squeezed my balls, and I gasped at the pleasure coursing through me. Game up. She knew I was awake now.

"Good morning," I said, grinning.

Rising from my cock, her gaze met mine.

"It will be." She took me deep again.

Damn. Her mouth was pure torture—if one considered pleasure torture. She sucked me deep, then ran her tongue up one side to the head and down the other, before taking me deep into her mouth again. My balls tightened.

Her fingers circled the base of my dick. If she kept sucking me like this, I would explode in her mouth. Did she want that? Could she handle that? Not all women could. Cassie didn't stop. She continued to stroke and suck me. Her fingers trailed to my balls and then lower. Her finger was at my ass.

She wouldn't dare. Would she? Before the thought left my mind, she pressed her finger inside my ass.

"Fuck!" The word escaped my lips as I stiffened with the blast of a powerful climax. I began spurting in her mouth as pure ecstasy filled me. Damn, this woman was lethal.

When I came down from my high, I glanced at her and saw the cocky grin on her face. I shook my arms. "Time to release me."

"Nope." She slid off the bed and sauntered over to the bathroom doorway.

"What the fuck do you mean, no?" While I'd allowed her to restrain me this one time—well, okay, she managed to do it without my permission—I'd had enough. I wanted to touch her, kiss her, fuck her.

"I'll release you when I'm done with you. Besides, I don't know your safe word." She sauntered into the bathroom.

I lay there stunned. She wasn't going to release me, and she didn't know my safe word? I didn't fucking have one, because I hadn't needed one since my early twenties when I was learning about BDSM.

My dick twitched. "Cassie," I yelled. "Get the fuck back in here and let me loose!"

"Wow, I thought waking up to a blow job would mellow you out." She strolled to the bed, a washcloth and towel in her hands.

Oh shit. She was going to clean me up. My cock was ready for a second round so this wasn't going to be pretty. "Baby, please untie me."

"Later." She stroked the warm washcloth over my chest, then dried me with the fluffy towel.

There had to be a way out of these cuffs. The warmth enveloped my cock as she cleaned me up the way I had done for her yesterday. Not that I didn't appreciate the gesture, but damn it, I was the one who was supposed to be in control.

Her touch was gentle, and once she finished bathing my balls, my dick stood up, begging for attention. I had to force myself not to struggle against the restraints. I knew exactly how strong they were—I'd made sure of it.

I breathed a sigh of relief when she finished drying me off. She tossed the towel aside, then straddled me.

"What shall I do with you now?" She ran her nails up and down my hard cock, sending shivers of exhilaration though me.

"Release me and I'll show you." My voice was husky with need.

"You have a one-track mind."

"I do. And right now, the only thought I have is being freed and fucking you until you can't move."

She laughed. I realized, right then, I was seeing yet another side of Cassie. While she'd been playful before, this was different. She'd taken control and let her sensual side out to play, and she wasn't afraid.

I sucked in a breath when she leaned over, trapping my hardness between our bodies. She gave me a soft kiss before her lips trailed down my neck to my chest. She took one of my nipples in her mouth, and my back arched.

Fuck. I'd never had a woman suck my nipples. Never cared to have anyone do it, but with Cassie, desire shot straight to my groin. Fire swept through my veins as she shifted to my other nipple. The blood rushed from my brain to my cock.

My balls tightened. Damn it, this woman was going to throw me over the edge without even touching my dick. For my entire life, I'd been in control. I came when I was ready; I hardened because I wanted to be turned on.

With Cassie, all that had gone out the window. I was at her mercy and not at all sure how I felt about that.

Well, physically, I knew.

I wiggled beneath her, trying to find a way I could slide myself into her slick pussy, but she'd positioned herself too well. I couldn't shift enough to thrust into her.

"Baby." I groaned when she alternated licking and sucking my nipples. My nipples had never been that sensitive.

Maybe it was the woman paying them attention that made them so needy.

"It's hard to explain." She sat up, staring at me. "You taste like a man, all masculine." She leaned down and gave my chest another lick, then smiled. "A little salty, but not unpleasant, and with an underlying muskiness."

Her words heated my blood, and damn if my cock wasn't pulsing with need. "If you don't get your hot, wet cunt on my dick, I'm going to come without being inside you."

"And that's a bad thing?" She wiggled her body over my trapped cock, teasing me with her soft silky skin.

Oh, just wait until I was free. I was going to torment the hell out of her.

"Cassie."

"I love it when you groan my name like that." Her nipples brushed against mine, and I gritted my teeth. "I love having you under my control, and while I know you'd rather be the one in control, it's my turn to pleasure you."

"Fuck, woman. Don't you realize your pleasure is mine?" Was that even my voice? That raw sound? "Put my dick in your pussy and ride me."

"Later." She took my mouth with hers.

This was one thing I could control. When her tongue tangled with mine, I captured it and wouldn't let it go. It didn't seem to faze her as she kissed me back, and her body undulated over mine. My skin had turned hypersensitive. When she broke the kiss, our heavy breathing filled the room. My balls were tight against my body.

"Honey, if you don't fuck me right now, I'm going to come all over both of us. Do you really want to waste that?" I kept my tone as even as I could.

"Oh." Her eyes grew wide. "No, I don't want to waste that." She adjusted herself. My hands jerked at the cuffs when she held my dick. "Nice and hard." She stroked me from tip to root with her hand.

There was no way to prevent the moan that left my lips. Then she squeezed my tip.

"Fuck." My hips bucked what little they could in the restraints. "You're killing me."

"Not my intention." She nipped at my chest, and damn, if my cock didn't grow even harder. How much more could I take?

Finally, she positioned herself and sheathed my dick in her hot, moist pussy.

"Shit!" I struggled with the cuffs. She'd only taken the tip of me inside her. "Move." I tried to force more of myself into her, but the damn restraints held me back. When I got loose...

She took in another inch of me.

With a cat-like smile, she rose, only leaving my tip inside her. Then she slid back down, taking me deeper. "You're not in control now." She kissed my chin.

I gritted my teeth. "You think I don't know that?"

"I'm sure you do." She slowly lowered herself until she'd fully taken me in. Her pussy contracted around my dick, and I could only moan.

My moan of pleasure was short lived. Cassie put her hands behind her, putting more pressure on our groins, and arched her back. My body shook.

Her pelvis flexed ever so slightly against me. "You're so big."

I swore my dick grew bigger. Her pussy surrounded me with wet heat. My fingers curled into my palms.

Her eyes drifted shut, and a sense of contentment flowed through me at the look of rapture on her face. She was enjoying herself. This wasn't just about sex. This was about pure desire.

I'd found a rare woman, and I wasn't going to let her go. Before I could find the right words to speak, her pussy tightened, and she pressed her body against mine.

Oh, God, I was going to die right now. I couldn't thrust into her. I jerked my foot... It was loose. She must have released the restraints when she leaned back. Elation hit my blood stream. I tested my left leg, and it was loose as well.

Bending my knees, I found traction and arched up as she pressed down.

"Yessss," she cried out.

I met her every down stoke with an upward thrust, adding more and more force with each pass and going deeper than I ever have. "That's it baby. Fuck me." I'd never been so turned on or hard in my life.

Cassie placed her palms on my chest as she began to ride me hard and fast. I fought against my climax until she was ready. Her pussy tightened around my dick like a vise, and she cried out, "I'm going to come."

Her mouth opened on a scream as her orgasm swept over her. I finally let my own release loose, and my seed spurted into her. I could barely breathe with the force of my own climax.

Cassie fell forward against my chest, her breathing fast. My cock was still buried deep inside her. When the cuffs fell away from my wrists, I wiggled my arms, pleased to find they were in working order. I embraced her, holding her against my thudding heart, before I cupped her chin and tilted her face up for a kiss.

"That was fun," she said after the kiss and pressing her cheek against my chest.

The smile in her voice caused me to grin. "Now, it's my turn." I rolled her onto her back, my cock stirring within her pussy. Greedy boy.

"Again?" she asked.

"What do you think?" I flexed my hips, and she let out a sexy groan.

"You're insatiable."

"So are you." I took her lips in another kiss as I began to move. I wasn't gentle. I thrust hard and fast. Cassie took everything I had to give her, screaming her second release in seconds. But I kept going. This woman would take everything I gave her and still come back from more.

I'd met my match.

Chapter Twenty-Nine

♥

Marcus

"Why are we getting out of bed?" Cassie asked several hours later.

"There is something I want to show you." I pulled her to her feet. While we'd lain in each other's arms, in the afterglow of yet another earth-shattering climax, I knew I wanted to show her my special room.

Taking her hand, I pulled her out of the bedroom.

"Wait a second." She tugged me to a stop.

"What?" Now that I'd made the decision to show her the room, I was impatient to see her reaction.

"I need my robe."

"No, you don't."

"Marcus." The exasperation in her tone made me smile.

"We're the only two people in the house. Besides, I like having you naked and ready for me."

Her cheeks turned pink, and I couldn't help but grin. With all we'd done together, she could still blush. I loved it. Leaning down, I brushed a kiss against her lips, then tugged her out of the room and down the hall. At the door, I punched a code into the electronic lock.

"Why is this room locked?"

"Long story, I'll explain later." I'd put an electronic lock on the room when an old girlfriend broke into my home and this special play room. She'd ruined several thousand dollars' worth of stuff before the police arrived.

I slipped my arm around Cassie's waist and guided her into the room, waiting until we were deep within the dark space before saying the command to turn the lights on. I kept my gaze on her face, not surprised to see her eyes widen, her lips compress, and her arms cross over her breasts. Had this been the wrong move?

She slipped out of my hold and walked over to the leather-padded bench. "Oh, my goodness." She ran the pads of her fingers seductively over the supple material before moving to the swing suspended from the ceiling.

I watched as she padded around the room, her feet almost silent against the highly polished floor. I kept my gaze on her, judging every little nuance. She didn't seem repelled by the room, more curious.

Could she accept this was a part of me? Or would she walk away because of it?

"Your special room?" She glanced over her shoulder at me, her breathing rapid.

"Yes." I moved to join her. "Explore the room all you want." Then I commanded, "Unlock all cabinets." I wanted her to have access to everything—I would keep nothing hidden from her.

As locks clicked open, she jumped and stared at me.

"The room is voice controlled, set to my voice only. Helpful if I only have one hand free."

"Another one of your R&D projects?" She strode over to the sixth cabinet and opened the door.

"I'm very creative in my R&D work." I forced myself to stand still, but watched her carefully. From what she'd shared with me, I didn't want her to panic. Not now. All I could do was hope she didn't. While I hadn't used everything in this room yet, I loved my collection of BDSM toys and equipment.

There were six cabinets, and the sixth one was about half full of whips and paddles. Her soft gasp filled the room, and I couldn't stop myself from moving to her side. My arm curved around her waist, anchoring her to my side. A small tremor shook her frame.

"Spanking cabinet." It wouldn't have been the first one I wanted her to look at, but I wasn't going to hide anything from her. I'd allow her to discover what appealed to her.

Chapter Thirty

♥

Cassie

I swallowed while staring at the implements inside the cabinet, glad Marcus was holding me. Of course, I'd picked the implement cabinet first. Blind luck. What had my mother found so fascinating about being hurt by these things?

Memories of my mother's screams filled my head, and I pushed them away. Marcus wasn't like my father.

Riding crops of every shape and size, canes, whips, and several other items I'd only seen in the Fantasies, Inc. catalogs. It was part of my job to know what the company offered.

"I'm not into pain." I forced the words past the lump in my throat.

"Neither am I." He reached past me, pulled out a black-handled flogger, and ran it over my arm. Gooseflesh popped out on my skin. The falls of the flogger were covered in velvet. They stroked my skin like a lover's touch.

"This is one of my favorites." He ran the falls across my breasts, causing my nipples to harden. "Soft and supple, it caresses the skin even if I use it on your body."

He snapped the implement against my hip. I jumped, but from surprise not pain. There was only a slight thump, but nothing harmful. And pleasure zinged through my veins, a reaction I didn't expect. "I created this one to entice and pleasure, not hurt."

"And the others?" I held back a moan when he ran the falls over my breasts a second time, teasing my nipples with the velvet.

"Some are made to warm your ass, but only if you want it."

I bit my lower lip.

"Don't get nervous, my love." His finger caressed my lower lip, coaxing me to release it. "I haven't used them in years."

"But the leather ones look well kept." My stomach tightened. How many other women had he entertained in this room?

"I spend time keeping the leather supple, but that doesn't mean I use them."

"And the other cabinets?"

"Go find out."

He put the flogger back in its place, yet I couldn't move. My mind was filled with apprehension and anticipation as I remembered another time and place.

"Go investigate," he said when I hadn't moved. He gave me a light swat on my ass. It jolted me out of my dark thoughts.

"Bossy." I flashed him a tentative smile, then went to the next cabinet. An unusual anticipation thrummed through my veins as I pulled the door open.

Sex toys. Dildos, vibrators, cock rings, pumps, bullets—all toys known to man and probably more than a few of Marcus' R&D prototypes.

I shivered with the thoughts of all the fun we could have with these items. I glanced over my shoulder to see Marcus grinning at me. He was probably thinking the same thing I was.

I moved to the next cabinet. All the items one needed for anal play. I wasn't sure if I was ready to investigate that, yet I'd tapped Marcus' ass when I sucked him off.

Hmm, I needed to think about that. I moved on to the next cabinet.

This one held oils and body paint, along with adult DVDs, and items for restraining a person. My blood pumped hard through my veins, and my pussy moistened.

Marcus was a man with hidden depths, and I wanted to explore each and every one of them. Too bad we only had the rest of today and tonight to discover those depths.

Finished with the cabinets, I made my way around the room. Rings were drilled into the walls and ceiling, some holding restraints and others not. There was a massive bed in the room as well, its metal frame imposing. Restraints were attached to the headboard and footboard.

Hot molten lava heated my blood as I wondered how quickly Marcus could tie me up and fuck me.

Probably pretty fast.

It was interesting that my apprehension was gone, and in its place, excitement. It had to be because I trusted Marcus. Each time I'd said my safe word, he stopped and talked with me. He listened to me and my fears.

When I said I wasn't into pain, he'd said he wasn't either. He wanted to give pleasure. Oh, that flogger might have seemed a little scary at first, but I was amazed at how good it felt. Nothing more than a deep massage.

I needed to think on this. So different from what I remembered growing up. I hadn't reconciled the two in my head yet, but another part of me really wanted to ignore my past. It was just that: the past.

Marcus was different. He wasn't pushing me into anything; he was leading me down the path, and it was up to me to take it. And I wanted to take it. I was tired of hiding.

Maybe, in time, we could have more than just this weekend.

Chapter Thirty-One

♥

Marcus

I watched Cassie tour my version of a BDSM dungeon. Long ago, I knew I'd rather play in private than in public.

Her face revealed very little, and that was unusual. Was she disgusted? I couldn't tell. Her skin was flushed, maybe she was embarrassed?

She hadn't been embarrassed by anything we'd done so far. Was my special room too much for her? She approached me, her gaze at her feet.

My heart pounded. If she couldn't accept this side of me, we'd be in real trouble. I needed, no wanted, a woman who would embrace her sexuality and mine, not hide from it. Cassie and I had made great progress over the last few days, and I wanted—no, I *needed* her to accept all of me and accept everything she was.

"Cassie?" I couldn't stand her silence any longer. My fingers curled into my palms to prevent myself from touching her. I wanted her to make the decision without any influence from me.

"I never..." The hesitation in her voice caused my heart to drop to my feet.

My hands clenched tighter. "It's okay. Let's go back to the bedroom." I spun around, my hopes dashed. As much as I wanted to take her in my arms, I couldn't. Not in here, where she didn't want to be. Not when my heart was being ripped out of my chest.

"No!" She grabbed my arm and tugged at me to turn around.

Her eyes were bright and glassy.

"It's okay, Cassie." I cupped her cheeks with my palms when a tear or two slipped down her cheek. "I understand if you're not into this."

"Wrong." Her voice was soft as I brushed away the tears. "I never thought I'd find a man interested in helping me see the safe side of sexual exploration. That it wasn't all pain." Her voice trembled.

"You're shaking with fear."

"Yes and no." Her fingers encircled my wrist. "There's something you need to know."

I nodded. The room was warm so I led her over to the padded bench, because the bed was too tempting. A rock formed in my gut. Whatever she wanted to tell me wasn't good.

Sitting down on the bench, I pulled her onto my lap and waited. When she didn't speak, I asked, "Why the tears?" I brushed several more away.

"It's hard to explain." Her fingers entwined with mine. "I told you yesterday about my father blindfolding me to punish me."

The rock turned to a boulder the size of a mountain. "Yes. Did your father beat you?" That would explain a lot of her fear. I could barely get the words out, it hurt so much to think of that happening.

"Not me—my mother." She let out a sigh and rested her head against my shoulder. "I'm saying this all wrong."

"It's okay." I brought her hand to my lips and kissed each finger. "Tell it however you can." I needed to know.

"My mother is a submissive and possibly a masochist."

"And your father's a Dominant and a sadist." That much was obvious to me.

"Destructively so, for both of them. When I was little, I didn't understand why they'd go into a locked room all the time. It wasn't until I was older I realized what was going on."

"How old were you?" I couldn't imagine what she saw or heard as a child.

"Fifteen. I suspected something unusual was going on with my parents before that. Dad was always ordering Mom around, and she'd do whatever he wanted."

"But you didn't." Some of the pieces fell into place.

"I didn't. Worse, I rebelled. I resented his attitude, especially when I started dating. Each time I defied him, he'd blindfold me, tie my hands behind my back, and shove me into a closet."

"Bastard." I cradled her against me. It was a miracle she'd allowed me to restrain her. There was some amazing steel in her attitude.

"He never hurt me physically, but he exerted his control over me."

"And your mother?" The picture was becoming clearer.

"Yes, and as hard as it is for me to admit it, my mother liked it."

"Some women do." It sounded like, to me, her father was a sadist, and her mother a masochist.

Cassie raised her head from my shoulder and nodded. "One night when he locked me in the closet, I stopped panicking about my loss of sight and realized I could hear things. I figured out that he'd purposely locked me in that particular closet. It was right next to the room where he and my mom had sex. He wanted me to hear."

"A room like this?"

"Not really." Her gaze swept around the room before returning to me. There was no fear in her eyes, and her body was relaxed against mine. "One time, I managed to slip the blindfold up a little bit. The closet was empty, cold, and unfeeling. This room is anything but. It reflects the man who lives here, and he's anything but cold." She snuggled up to me.

Slowly, the boulder in my gut broke apart. "I'm glad you feel that way." I kissed her temple. "Do you want to finish your story?"

She sighed. "I peeked into their bedroom and saw there were benches where he could tie Mom up. This one night I could hear them. I heard him whipping her, and she was screaming. But she was also telling him to whip her harder, to hurt her while he fucked her."

"I would never—"

Her fingers against my lips stopped my words.

"I've come to believe you would never hurt me. I didn't understand their relationship until I read the book in your library last night about the submissive having power. My mother was a true submissive, but also a masochist. I was afraid that when it came to sex, I was going to be like her."

Her voice grew small. "All my adult life, I've been afraid. I don't ever want to be like that."

"How could you think that?" I shook my head, trying to get over the shock of her words. I turned her in my lap until she straddled me. "You are a bedroom submissive. Do you understand the difference?"

"I do, now." Her warm breath brushed against my skin. "Part of the problem is the men in my past freaked out when I suggested anything remotely kinky, so I always fell in with their wishes. Hence these thoughts that I was more submissive than I thought."

"They were idiots." I wanted to hunt down each one of those men and teach them a lesson, starting with her father.

"I began to wonder if I needed someone to dominate me in order for me to enjoy sex."

"You don't." My dominance was never about sex; it was about making sure my partner had pleasure.

"I know that now. You showed me what control really meant. We both have it, and we've brought each other pleasure with it."

I closed my eyes. Cassie didn't understand how her words affected me or the intense emotions they stirred up. I wasn't going to be able to let go tomorrow. I would fight tooth and nail to keep her in my life. I couldn't fail.

"So you're not turned off by my special room?"

"I'm excited, and at times, apprehensive." She took a breath. "While I'm not interested in the whips, canes, or implements like that, I think we can still have some fun together. I wouldn't mind if you tried spanking me with your hand." Her skin flushed.

"You liked it when I swatted your ass."

"I did."

"I can work with that." My lips covered hers in a soft kiss before I leaned back. "We'll build up to the spanking. But we can play with some of the other items in the cabinets, the ones that don't scare you." My lips turned up. "Or maybe ones that make you a little nervous but you're willing to try."

"Now that sounds like a lot of fun." She grinned at me. "Can we start now?"

Fuck. How did I deserve this woman? "Yes, we can."

Chapter Thirty-Two

♥

Cassie

Several hours later, I lazed in the bathtub. My muscles ached, heck, places of me ached I didn't even know I had. But it was a good ache. A grin tugged at my lips as I remembered the afternoon in Marcus' special room.

After playing all night and having so many orgasms, it was a wonder I could function or think. My breasts were tender; my pussy pulsed, and my heart burst with love for Marcus. A love I could never acknowledge to him.

I had one secret in my life that only I could deal with. Once I did, then maybe there would be hope for me and Marcus. If I told him about it, he'd want to defeat all my demons for me. Plus, I wasn't even sure I was ready to expose this last secret. Even in my own mind and heart, I buried it deep.

"Aren't you done yet?" A nude Marcus strode into the bathroom with two glasses of wine in his hands. I took one from him and took a sip.

"Almost." I sighed as the wine slid down my throat. "I'm not used to such vigorous exercise."

"Finish your bath, and I'll give you a massage." He took a drink from his glass, and I enjoyed the way he swallowed, his neck stretching and his Adam's apple shifting as the liquid slid down his throat. Lord, I was a goner.

"I do want you to answer something for me," he said. "Why do you keep hiding parts of yourself?"

I leaned my head against the tub, thinking. It wasn't a surprise he wanted answers, but I wasn't ready to give them to him, not yet. I could tell him a few things, though.

"My last relationship went sour very quickly when I expressed my interest in something other than the missionary position, and I tried to introduce some toys into the bedroom." I sighed. "That didn't go over well."

"Jackass."

I laughed because Marcus made me feel better. "Yeah. I decided to save myself from future hurt, so I built up a defense against my sexuality and my needs."

"A damn hard wall that took me forever to beat down." He set his empty wine glass on the counter. "Are you coming out or do I join you?"

Relief poured through me. He wasn't going to question me more. Thank goodness. I was nowhere ready to confess all. Handing him my empty glass, I rose from the cooling water.

Marcus held a warm towel out. I was going to miss being pampered. But all good things must come to an end. "How many people know about your special room?"

"Four. Including you."

I blinked in surprise. "That's not very many." Had women run screaming when they saw it? He had to have brought women here before.

"There's the builder, you, myself, and an ex-girlfriend."

The way he said ex-girlfriend made me shiver. Something had happened, and it wasn't good. Dread spread its icy fingers over my heart.

Not toward Marcus. I knew him well enough by now to know he didn't do something to trigger some sort of event.

"What did the ex do?" I smoothed my fingers over the frown marring his forehead.

He pulled me into his arms. "I ended my relationship with her, and she wasn't happy. She broke into the house and then into my special room and trashed it."

"That explains all the security." I couldn't blame him. What a horrible thing to happen.

"Yes. I will never allow something like that to happen again." He paused. "It was a long time ago." He swept me off my feet and into his arms, and I squealed. "I'm tired of all this serious talk," he said. "Time to give you a massage." He carried me into the bedroom.

Not only did he give me a massage, but showed me a night I would never forget.

If only I could stay.

Chapter Thirty-Three

♥

C assie

I slipped from bed, fighting back the tears filling my eyes. Walking across the room, I slid the bathroom door almost closed. I gathered up my clothes I'd put in there earlier and dressed. I couldn't even look at myself in the mirror. If I did, I'd see the love I couldn't acknowledge or share.

Marcus made love to me for hours before we fell asleep, and even as exhausted as I was, I'd only slept a couple hours. I'd spent the last hour lying on my side watching him.

Everything I'd fought against came true. My heart was lost to him, and there wasn't a damn thing I could do about it. Now, the fantasy was over. It was Monday morning.

I squirmed against the constriction of my clothing. I'd become accustom to being naked. Finding the pen and paper I stashed with my clothing, I wrote Marcus a note. I'd known yesterday I would have to write him this morning. I couldn't just leave.

Once I finished, I picked up my packed bag and turned out the light in the bathroom before I opened the door. Funny, the darkness didn't bother me as much as it had before. Marcus had left the curtains open, so the moonlight spilled into the room.

I placed the note on the dresser and set my bag by the door. I quietly made my way over to the bed where Marcus softly snored. There, I carefully picked up his phone and held it to his face. It unlocked the phone and I turned off his alarm. I didn't want it to wake him before I was gone. Guilt hit me at making him late for work, but it had to be done.

I allowed myself a moment to stand there, staring down at him. His face was relaxed, his mouth slightly parted, his legs spread, and his cock semi-erect. I'd never find another man like him, and I didn't want to. Marcus was one of a kind. If only—

No. I would never be the woman he wanted. My inability to sleep and my bad dreams would make it impossible. So that was that.

The clock on his bedside clicked to six a.m. I brushed away the tears running down my cheeks before I leaned down and brushed a light kiss over his lips.

"Be well, Marcus, and know that I love you."

With a heavy heart, I straightened, walked to the door, picked up my bag, and stepped outside the bedroom.

I couldn't stop myself from glancing back at him. My fantasy weekend was over, but in my heart, I'd never love another man the way I loved Marcus.

Chapter Thirty-Four

♥

Marcus

I groaned and rolled over as my cell kept ringing. Who the hell was calling me so early?

I found my cell and answered without looking at it. "What the hell do you want?" It was too darn early to be civil.

"It's Josh. It's not like you to be late, so I was elected to check on you."

Late? It was like a bucket of cold water was thrown over me. I sat up and stared at the clock.

Nine? What the *hell*? Had I slept through my alarm? I planned on making love to Cassie before we went into the office together.

"Sorry I yelled. I overslept. I'll be in the office shorty." I tossed my cell back on the nightstand and turned to Cassie. The space beside me was empty, the sheets cold. I cocked my head, listening.

Silence.

Cassie was gone.

Pain and sorrow squeezed my heart. Why had she left? Why sneak off? Hadn't she learned yet we could get through anything together? Confusion swirled through my mind. While this had only been for the weekend, I'd expected her to stay.

Anger rushed through my veins. Why would she leave? Admittedly, the time we'd negotiated was up, but I didn't tell her to go. I wanted her to stay. I grabbed my cell and found my alarm had been switched off.

Cassie must had turned it off, but why?

"Damn it." I swung my legs off the bed.

After the awesome fucking time we'd had yesterday—hell, all weekend— I was sure she would've understood I didn't want what we had to end. Apparently, my thinking was flawed.

She had to be at work. The second the staff meeting with Josh's group was over, I'd find her, lock her in my office, and not let her go. At least, not until she explained herself.

I stalked to the dresser and yanked open the drawer, catching sight of the envelope bearing my name. I ripped it open and began to read.

Marcus, our weekend together was the most wonderful experience of my life and one I will never forget, but it was just for the weekend. It's now over. It's time for us to move on with our lives. I wish you all the best.

My temper grew until it was a living flame inside of me.

This wasn't over. Not by a long shot. If Cassie thought I'd let her go that easily, she was mistaken.

She was mine for yesterday, today, and always, and I wouldn't accept anything less.

Chapter Thirty-Five

♥

Cassie

I placed the lid on the box sitting on my desk. There hadn't been a lot to clean out of my office. I didn't keep a lot of personal things there.

"I can't believe you're leaving," Lisa, my assistant, said.

"Time for me to move on." I shrugged. While showering this morning, I'd made the decision to leave Fantasies, Inc. It hadn't been easy, but there was no way I could see Marcus every day and not break down.

It was better this way. I bottled up my emotions. I'd sworn my staff to secrecy until I could talk with the President Boyd and hand in my resignation personally. Yes, I could have chickened out and just sent an email to HR. But I couldn't. I owed it to the president to tell him in person, especially since I was leaving without notice.

I glanced at my watch. Ten-twenty. I was due in the president's office at ten-thirty. Picking up my letter of resignation, I crossed over to Lisa. "I want you to know I've recommended you to Mr. Boyd as my replacement."

Lisa looked stunned. "But—"

"You deserve it." I walked past my stunned assistant to the elevators. Marcus had a meeting with Josh's department. He'd let that slip yesterday, so I timed everything out to avoid him. If I saw him... I didn't have a clue what I would do.

My heart dropped to my feet as the elevator whisked me to the top floor. While this was for the best, I couldn't help but be sad. I was going to miss my job and the people I worked with. Jackie, Mr. Boyd's executive assistant smiled at me when I walked in. "Go on in; he's waiting for you."

"Thanks." I took a deep breath before knocking on the door and entering.

"Cassie, you're always so punctual." Mr. Boyd rose to his feet.

I stopped in my tracks. There was someone sitting in front of his desk. "I'm sorry; Jackie said to come in. I can come back later."

"You will not take one step," a familiar voice commanded.

Shock at hearing Marcus' voice froze me in place. What the hell was he doing here?

"That's my cue to leave." Mr. Boyd crossed the room to me. "I'm going to tell you what I told Marcus: I'm not accepting your resignation. Work this out, and be sure to notify HR afterward if you choose to continue your relationship." Mr. Boyd stepped around me, opened the door, and closed it behind him.

My stomach clenched when Marcus stood and faced me. He was pissed.

Could I blame him? Not really. I did leave without saying good bye. But it was more than that. There was something in his features besides anger. Something I didn't dare put into words.

Chapter Thirty-Six

♥

Marcus

The second I saw Cassie, my anger flared hotter, then died instantly when I spotted the sadness in her features. My first reaction was to take her by the shoulders and kiss her, long and deep. I pushed my need down. We needed to have this discussion. If I couldn't convince her to stay, she'd slip from my fingers forever, and I refused to let that happen.

"Why did you leave me this morning, Cassie?" I fought to keep my tone level.

"It was time. Our weekend was over."

I eyed her up and down. Her cold tone sent chills through the air, but the agony in her eyes confused me. What was holding her back?

"We never had a chance to finish our talk," I said, carefully modulating my voice so she wouldn't hear the desperation behind my question.

"Excuse me?" Her eyes widened.

"You heard me. Cassie, I need to know. What are you so afraid of?" Where was the warm, passionate woman I held in my arms this weekend? This was a cold imitation, and I wasn't about to let Cassie get away with it. She'd shown me the sensual woman inside, and I'd be damned if I would let her bottle that woman up again.

Cassie stiffened. I was pushing her buttons, asking her what she was afraid of, but there was something she wasn't telling me, and we had to find a way past it.

The fire burning inside me, all for her, was out of control. We'd spent a wonderful weekend together, one I wanted to repeat over and over for the next sixty or seventy years, if this stubborn woman would let me.

"I'm not afraid of anything." She crossed her arms over her chest, the paper, which I assumed was her resignation, in her hand crackling against the pressure.

"Bullshit. You wouldn't have walked out this morning without saying good-bye if you weren't afraid." Did she not realize how much I'd studied her this weekend? Hell, even before then, but this weekend had given me so much more insight to this woman I loved.

I blinked. *I loved her.*

I hadn't realized that until this moment, yet now, looking back, I could see I'd been half in love with her before the weekend ever started.

"The deal was for sixty hours, and that's what you got." Anger sparked in her eyes.

Good. Get angry, be mad, and show me those emotions. Show me the passionate woman who isn't afraid. "I'm not talking about our agreement." I took a step and stopped, flexing my fingers at my sides so I wouldn't reach out and grab her. "Did I scare you in some way?" The question almost brought me to my knees. "Too much sex?" Was there such a thing? "Whatever has you frightened, we can work it out. Together."

And we could. I'd come to the realization instantly. I wanted her in my life, even if it meant vanilla sex, although I doubted kink was the issue.

"There is nothing to work out. I told you in my note: You had your weekend. End of story."

"Bullshit."

I rubbed the back of my neck, wondering how to get through to her. Having our deal thrown in my face wasn't what I expected. I expected her to be honest with me and herself.

Enough.

I took her by shoulders, driven by the need to touch her. "After everything we shared this weekend, you still want to end our relationship?"

"It was sex. Nothing else."

I almost believed her until her gaze skittered away from mine. Hope flared inside me. She was fighting. "It was more than sex to me." I gentled my hold and my tone.

Cassie didn't say a word.

"This weekend was way more than sex—it was about the woman I want to keep in my life." It was it all up to her.

"Marcus." Her stance relaxed, and her voice trembled.

"I told you I only wanted the weekend, but that was a lie. I want more. If you walk away from me now, my life will be empty. I love you, and there is nothing I'd like to do more than prove that to you."

She tore herself from my hold and turned her back to me. Had I lost her? Loss hit me in the gut worse than any sucker punch. I never failed. Through my college years, I had a professor who said I'd never amount to anything but failure. In spite of him, I thrived. There was a first time for everything, but I wished it wasn't something as critical as convincing the love of my life to stay, to give us a chance.

Before now, I never stopped a woman from walking away if that's what she wanted, but this was different. This was Cassie. I'd put it all on the line, telling her how I felt. There was nothing more I could do.

Her silence was killing me. Apparently, she would stick to her decision. I hung my head, unable to fathom a dreary life without Cassie in it. I couldn't stay. Couldn't look at her any longer and know she would never be mine.

Without a word, I stepped around her and reached for the door.

"No!" Her fingers curled around my wrist.

I froze, unsure how many more blows I could take before I crumbled at her feet and begged.

"I love you too." Her words were soft, but the breath she took in after them was ragged with emotion. "There's something else I need to tell you."

My muscles tightened even more as I waited. When she didn't speak, I glanced over my shoulder. There were tears in her eyes—the emotions she'd kept bottled up were breaking free.

Thank God.

"Don't cry, sweetheart." I turned and gathered her into my arms. I couldn't stand seeing her cry, especially since I was the cause of her tears.

"I can't help it." She buried her face against my shirt. "I'm so afraid."

"Of what?"

She trembled in my embrace. "That I can never be the woman you want me to be."

I was struck speechless for a moment. "What kind of woman do you think I want?" Where the hell was this coming from? How could she think that? She was perfect for me.

"A submissive."

"What the fuck?" I held her at arm's length. "Where the hell did you get that idea from?"

"Come on, Marcus, this whole weekend was about control—you controlling me. You let me be the aggressor once, but the rest was all you. Even your special room reeks of a Dominant and his submissive. You say you only want me submissive in bed, but that will change."

She really believed that? Her features were tight. There had to be more. "You are no submissive," I said.

And that was the truth. She was a sexual submissive most of the time, but really she was a switch. She liked to dominate on her terms.

"I won't be like my mother." She continued as if she hadn't heard me. "I will not submit my life choices to your whim. I will not become a slave, and I sure as hell won't allow a man to almost kill me." She pulled herself from my embrace, and her hand covered her mouth.

The last piece of the puzzle fell into place. Her father's abusive tendencies, her insistence that she wasn't a submissive, her need for control. I hadn't put it all together until now. "What happened?" I reached for her, but she avoided me and marched over to the window to look out.

"It was the week I turned eighteen. I don't know what set my father off, but he took Mom into their play room. He'd already tied me up and put me in the closet, close enough where I heard everything. I could hear her screaming, but there was something different in her screams this time."

She rested her forehead against the glass, and I could barely stop myself from going over to her. Cassie looked as if she'd shatter into a million pieces if I touched her.

"She kept begging him to stop. She'd never done that before. I started kicking the wall, trying to get his attention. But he didn't stop. I started screaming at the top of my lungs. A neighbor heard me and called the police. By the time they arrived, my mother was unconscious and barely breathing."

"They arrested your father?" Even with the Sexual Freedom Act, the police would react to spousal abuse first, not matter what her father said. There was no tolerance for abuse.

"Yes, but Mom refused to press charges." She laughed bitterly.

My heart tightened. My poor Cassie.

"She told the police their sex play got out of hand, but she couldn't explain why I was tied up in the closet. I was still under eighteen, but I turned of age while she was in the hospital. I begged her to leave him. I left home the day she told me she was picking my father up from jail."

"Baby, you have to know I'd never do that." I touched her waist, watching her reflection in the glass. "Your father abused you and your mother."

"He did, and I will never put myself in that situation. I won't be submissive. I won't allow a man to beat me up like my father did to my mother. I won't let anyone tie up my child."

My heart hurt for the young woman Cassie had been and the horror she'd seen and experienced. I cupped her chin and turned her face to me. "Our children will be cherished, not punished the way you were. I love you, Cassie." When she opened her mouth, I touched her lips to quiet her words. "Listen to me as I say this again. You are a sexual submissive, meaning you like the man to take the lead in the bedroom. Not always, but most of the time. That's fine with me. I don't need someone who is submissive in all things. I don't want that. I want to laugh and argue and live normal lives. Cassie, I love you just the way you are."

There was doubt in her blue eyes. That wouldn't do.

"What if I can never do some of the things you want to do? There are some things I'll never want to do or try, like being blindfolded."

"It makes no difference." It didn't, not to me. I drew her against me. "I love you. I don't care if you want to spend the rest of our lives having nothing but vanilla sex. I can deal with it. As long as I have you in my bed, in my arms, in my life, I'll be a happy man."

Tears fell down her cheeks. I leaned over and kissed them away. "You make me happy, Cassie. Please, come home with me."

"I think we can be a little kinkier than vanilla." Her lips turned up, the first ray of hope I'd seen all day.

The knot in my gut unraveled. It was time to finish this conversation right. "I think we should conclude this the way we started." I took her hand, led her from John's office to the elevator, and then to my office. Once inside, I locked the door and pulled a small box out of my pocket. Dropping to one knee, I held the open box up to her.

"Cassie Adams, will you do me the honor of wearing these?"

Her gasp was loud in the room. Inside the box were a set of non-piercing gold nipple rings. They were for her to wear as she wanted until I could get her a real ring for her finger. "Oh, Marcus." The love shining from her eyes brought joy to my heart. "Yes."

With a wide smile, I stood and pulled her into my arms. "Until you're ready to have my ring on your finger, these rings will signify my commitment to you and only you."

She laughed. "Only you would seal the agreement with nipple rings."

"I am special." I brushed a kiss against her lips. "But not as special as the woman I'm holding in my arms."

"I love you so much." She buried her face against my chest.

"Me too. So what do you say we get the ball rolling and you move into my place tomorrow?"

"Give you an inch and you take a mile." Her laughter rang through my office. "I'd like that."

"Done. But don't expect a lot of negotiations in your future."

"Oh?" She tilted her head as she gazed at me.

"I intended to make sure you're too sexually satisfied to argue with me."

"Sounds good to me." She drew my mouth down to hers to seal the deal.

***

I hope you've enjoyed Marcus and Cassie's story. Please leave a review where every you feel comfortable, this really helps me as the author reach more readers. Next up is Asher and Emma's story.

Asher is the head of IT at Fantasies, Inc. and Emma because a contractor to incorporate her software with Asher's. Forced proximity pushes these two together day after day. Sexual tension runs high, and a hacker cause trouble. Asher and Emma work together to protect the company and their love.

You can preorder Decoding Emma now. Go to http://www.marietuhart.com

Preview of Decoding Emma

♥

N ote: This is an unedited version

Emma

I sat in my small car in the warm spring air trying to convince myself to get out. Why was I so nervous?

My boss sent me over to Fantasies, Inc. to help customize the software I'd built into their system. I'd asked why I couldn't do it at Tri-O-Tech like I did all my work, but apparently the guy in charge of the technology department was a control freak and insisted all customization be done at his office.

A sigh escaped. I hated being in a place I didn't know. Some would say I was an introvert, and sometimes I was. I just liked being by myself and doing my own thing without people looking over my shoulder.

"Come on, Emma, get your ass out of the car." The pep talk helped me open the door and step out. The spring sun was warm on my skin. I opened the back door, pulled my backpack with my laptop out, then closed and locked my car.

I sucked in a breath and walked toward the building. The sun gleamed off the shiny windows as I glanced up at the logo. A smile crossed my lips. A big red heart with devil's horns the company name—Fantasies, Inc.—graced the building.

This job had come up so quickly I hadn't had time toinvestigate the company before I walked in. My boss called me at seven this morning and told me to be here by nine. Since I lived outside of Seattle, that meant driving right into West Seattle and dealing with all the traffic. My boss hinted that doing this job would help me get the promotion I craved. It also meant stepping out of my comfort zone.

I stepped off to the side of the automatic doors so as not to block the others from walking into the building. Some of them glanced at me and smiled, then continued on their way. They all seemed very relaxed and comfortable.

Those walking into the building were wearing a lot of different outfits. I glanced down at my black slacks and purple blouse. They were neat and clean. Yes, I was wearing sneakers, but I wanted to be comfortable. I fit right in. Taking a deep breath, I gave myself another peptalk, then stepped through. The coolness of the building's air condition wafted over my skin.

The lobby was nicely decorated. Sofas and chairs were spread around with small side tables. There were a few people waiting, probably meeting someone. There was a large reception area where my attention was caught on a man, standing tall, with the woman sitting behind the desk.

Another deep breath and I made my way over to the desk. The man glanced up. Our gazes locked. I stopped breathing. His green eyes were assessing, and I couldn't help feeling like I lacked something he was searching for. I adjusted my backpack and forced a smile.

"You must be Emma Palmer," the man said, holding out his hand. "I'm Asher Donahue, head of Technology here at Fantasies, Inc."

"Mr. Donahue." I shook his hand and heat invaded my veins. I took in his short dark hair, and the slight scruff on his face. While he wasn't in a suit, his pants and dress shirt looked expensive. A shaft of awareness slid through my body.

"Call me Asher."

"Emma." I pulled my hand away from his, but my gaze stayed on him. Why did he look familiar? He shouldn't.

"Our first stop is HR so we can get you set up." He cupped my elbow, and damn, if my pulse didn't skip a beat or two.

You can preorder Decoding Emma at https://www.marietuhart.com

About the author

♥

Marie Tuhart lives in the beautiful Pacific Northwest with her two dogs, Tommy and Trina. Marie brings to life contemporary approachable alpha heroes and the spunky women who take them to task. Her high-heat, emotional books, many with BDSM elements, inviting the reader to slid the silky scarves between their fingers, fell the kiss of a flogger on their flesh in breathless anticipation of what or who will come next. Embrace the temptation and enjoy a happily ever after that's always about the heroine.

Check out Marie's website at: https://www.marietuh art.com

Other Books by Marie Tuhart

Tempt *(Wicked Sanctuary Series)*

Entice *(Wicked Sanctuary Series)*

Seduce *(Wicked Sanctuary Series)*

Ravish *(Wicked Sanctuary Series)*

Possess *(Wicked Sanctuary Series)*

Tantalize *(Wicked Sanctuary Series)*

Edged *(Wicked Sanctuary Series)*

Unmasked *(Wicked Sanctuary Series)*

Too Hot *(Wicked Sanctuary Series)*

Wicked Sanctuary Novellas:

Untamed

Power Play

Claiming Rose

Standalone Books:

Embracing Desire

Broken Rules

Tangled Temptation

www.ingramcontent.com/pod-product-compliance
Lightning Source LLC
Chambersburg PA
CBHW040525170726
48295CB00012B/344